T0146427

SPIES IN A
SMALL
TOWN

SPIES IN A SMALL TOWN

WILLIAM MARTIN

SPIES IN A SMALL TOWN

iUniverse books may be ordered through booksellers or by contacting:

iUniverse
1663 Liberty Drive
Bloomington, IN 47403
www.iuniverse.com
1-800-Authors (1-800-288-4677)

ISBN: 978-1-5320-5015-2 (sc)
ISBN: 978-1-5320-5016-9 (e)

Library of Congress Control Number: 2018905949

Print information available on the last page.

iUniverse rev. date: 07/03/2018

CONTENTS

To the old man who moved his mountain one shovelful at a time and who always encouraged me to do the same.

Also to my wife and family for putting up with me, and to my typist par excellence, Anita Spencer.

Philip Settecase, for providing the first reading of the manuscript, and offering his comments.

Sarah Kathleen, for her endless copying and support.

Aaron Patrick, as a reader.

Michael Joseph Kline, Emmeritus Associate Professor of History, Ohio University Zanesville, Teacher, EDUCATOR, and mentor to me, and to many.

Any resemblance to any persons living or dead is purely coincidental.

Diane Smith arrived home at a quarter to five in the evening. She parked her Porsche in the back of the house where she rented an upstairs apartment. After she turned off the engine, quelling the throaty rumble, she gathered her briefcase and exited the car. Zane Winston, her boss and lover, would be stopping by on his way home from the family-owned optical factory. She had worked for Zane for eight years, the last two as vice president. She knew he would be anxious to discuss the Hungarian delegation that had been visiting the factory the last two days. He would arrive between five thirty and six, and she had to take a shower and get ready for the other things Zane would want.

As she unlocked her door and ascended the long flight of steps into her living quarters, she thought about how to approach Zane regarding the Hungarians and the events of the last two days. When she got to the top of the stairs, she dropped her briefcase and folders, stepped out of her four-inch stilettos, and took off her blouse and bra, freeing her ample breasts from their long confinement. She felt relaxed and free in the June heat. Proceeding to the kitchen, she filled a glass with ice cubes, poured it half-full of gin, topped it off with Schweppes tonic water, added a slice of lemon, and took a long pull of the drink. "Oh, the drink of the gods," she said as she lit a Lucky Strike. The combination of the alcohol and the nicotine hitting her brain let her know she had achieved nirvana. Drink in one hand, Lucky in the other, she proceeded into her bedroom. She

1

unfastened her skirt, letting it drop to the floor. Sitting on the edge of her bed, she unfastened her garters and rolled her stockings down her long, shapely legs. Standing once again, she unfastened the garter belt, letting it drop to the floor. As she peeled her panties down, she felt the breeze coming through the bedroom window. It engulfed her nude body. Diane took another drag on the Lucky, followed by a sip of gin. Then she stopped. She listened carefully, trying to identify the unusual noise she heard in her closet. Every cell in her being became alert. She softly sat her drink on the bedside stand, laid her Lucky Strike in the ashtray, and eased open the drawer of the bedside stand. She retrieved the Walther PP from the drawer. Her trained instincts told her to aim the 7.65 automatic at the closet. But before she could speak, the louver door burst open, and Carl Waters, the government assassin, appeared. He fired three shots from his silenced Smith & Wesson Model 10, striking her in and about her left breast. Diane was able to fire once, barely missing Carl's head, before she dropped backward dead onto the bed.

Thomas Atherton exited the living room closet where he had been hiding and raced into the bedroom. "Damn, that shot might alert the neighborhood. Couldn't you have shot more quickly?"

"Hey, I did the best I could. She armed herself and was ready."

"Okay, okay," Thomas replied. "Let's listen for the neighbors and see if anyone was disturbed. We don't want local cops snooping around." With that, the two assassins went from window to window observing the neighborhood. The neighborhood was quiet.

Carl and Thomas returned to the bedroom where Diane's body lay on the bed in a pool of blood. Carl said, "Man, what a beautiful piece of ass. Such a waste."

"She was an agent, an enemy of our country," Atherton, the true believer, said. "Now pull yourself together because we have two more."

"I know, I know. Let's get this finished and get back to Washington."

They waited for forty-five minutes until they heard the door open and then close at the foot of the stairs. They repositioned themselves in the living room to have access to the staircase. Zane Winston was about halfway up, saying, "Hey, Diane, it's me, Zane. Where are you?" Atherton moved to the top of the steps. He leveled his Model 10 snub-nosed silenced revolver and fired twice, striking Winston in the forehead and in the upper-left quadrant of the chest. Zane Winston pitched forward and dropped, his body flying down a few steps before coming to rest in a lifeless mass. The two assassins, who chose not to wear gloves, quickly rubbed the closet doors and anywhere else they might have touched and carefully exited the apartment.

"What about the scientist? He's the one the colonel seemed adamant about us taking out," Carl said.

"He's not here," Thomas said. "Maybe a change of plans. I don't know. But I do know we can't wait around for him. Let's get out of here."

"Okay, I'm all for that, but the colonel won't be happy."

They walked through the alley to the next street where their rented car was parked. The two assassins drove to the Putnam Landing airport, where they approached the ticket counter of Lake Central Airlines. They purchased two one-way tickets to Washington, DC, and arranged for the rental car to be picked up. At six thirty, they boarded the DC 47 and left Putnam Landing.

Sylvia Winston held dinner as long as she could, but by seven o'clock, the children were starving, so she let them eat. By the time they finished their meal, had their baths, and were in bed, Sylvia's slow burn with her husband had turned to rage. The rage was fueled by bourbon, and by ten o'clock, she was fitfully sleeping on the sofa in the living room. Sylvia was accustomed to Zane's late nights; they had been occurring off and on during their marriage. However, since he had promoted Diane Smith, the vice president of operations, the late nights had become more regular. She felt sure that the auburn-haired lady beauty was the cause of that. Nevertheless, she was too insecure about the possibility of losing her good life to confront the situation head-on. Instead, she found solace in freely spending large amounts of money and in alcohol.

Sylvia did not awaken until slightly after eight o'clock the next morning when the children, Brad, ten years old, and Caroline, eight years old, awoke her. She sat up slowly, her head throbbing as she struggled to her feet. "I'm sorry, kids, but Mommy fell asleep on the couch, and Daddy didn't wake me up. He must have had a late night. Is he upstairs?"

"No, Mom," Brad replied. "There's no one upstairs."

Sylvia, in her alcoholic fog, was trying to make sense of what she was hearing. Zane was not there. Maybe he had left early for the office. No, no, this was Saturday. The plant was closed. It was then that she knew he had not come home. She could barely conceal her rage. Through clenched teeth, she asked the children to go into the kitchen and have cereal and toast while she went upstairs to shower and get dressed. Listening to some dissension about Saturday morning and bacon and eggs, she firmly repeated her instructions and climbed the stairs.

Meanwhile, in another part of the city, Denise Potts was getting into her car. It was a quarter after nine, and she was on her way to pick up Diane Smith for a nine-thirty tennis match. Denise was a fourth-grade teacher in the Putnam Landing city schools. She and Diane had met three years before at a local bar and became friends. They both enjoyed tennis and tried to play at least once a week.

Denise pulled into the driveway of Diane's apartment at nine thirty, where she found Zane's Cadillac parked. "Oh dear," she said. "What do I do?"

Sylvia had cooled down after a long shower. She stood in front of the full-length bathroom mirror drying herself. She looked at the woman looking back at her and said, "Damn, you've still got it. Not bad for a thirty-six-year-old woman who's had two kids." The image staring back at her had natural raven-black hair, high cheekbones, deep blue eyes, and a body that wouldn't quit. Her breasts were still firm, with deep brown areolas and large nipples, her stomach flat, her full bush, the same color as the hair on her head, her legs long and tapered, and her feet adorned with bright toenail polish, courtesy of Molly Salon. "You combine this with a BA from Ohio University in Art History and you're still a catch. Damn him. I'll show that bastard that two can play this game." With that, she sat at her dressing table and began applying her makeup. Then it hit her. What if Diane Smith or another bimbo wasn't involved? What if something happened to Zane—something awful? What if he was in an accident and was lying in a ditch somewhere? What if he had been kidnapped or robbed and murdered? *Oh God*, she thought. She lit a Philip Morris, inhaled deeply, and contemplated what she should do next. Then she remembered Gabe.

Gabriel St. John was a classmate from high school who was now a detective on the Putnam Landing police force. They had had a brief fling in high school and once or twice while she was at Ohio University. He had a thing for her, but she could not take him seriously, as he had no ambitions in life. He could have attended Ohio State on a football scholarship but said that wasn't for him. He had been an outstanding linebacker at Putnam Landing High School, and Coach Damsel had worked to get him into the university, but Gabe just couldn't do it. And of course there was the war, and Gabe spent three years fighting Germans across most of Europe. When the war ended and he returned home, the relationship between him and Sylvia had cooled, mostly on her part. She could not understand why he didn't return to college after being in the army. Of course that meant he couldn't keep her in the style to which she was accustomed. Sylvia came from a very wealthy family in Putnam Landing; she knew the good life. Their family had not been touched by the Depression or by the war. In fact, the family profited from the war. So she just had been pretty much finished with Gabe until now.

She padded barefoot across the bedroom to the bedside table where she retrieved a phonebook from the drawer. She found the number for the Putnam Landing Police Department and dialed it.

"Detective St. John. How can I help you?"

"Gabriel, Gabe," Sylvia replied. "This is Sylvia Kelly Winston."

"Sylvia?" Gabe was quiet for a moment. "Sylvia, Sylvia, uh, well, what can I do for you?"

She briefly remembered what he had done for her in the past. Remembering their times together, she became aware of the moistness between her thighs. She then quickly returned to the present and said, "Gabe, Zane didn't come home last night. He never came home from work. I'm worried sick."

Gabe listened, but running through his mind was, *So, what's new?* Everyone in Putnam Landing knew of Zane Winston's reputation with women. It was the best open secret of all time.

Gabriel remembered that in eighth grade, Zane's parents had sent him away to some prep school and then to an Ivy League college. He returned to Putnam Landing and began working at Winston Optical with his father. Because of his father's political connections and the military contracts that Winston Optics had, his father had been able to get Zane a deferment from the draft.

Sylvia was feeling edgy, trying to hold back the tears that were welling up—tears of rage at Zane's infidelity, as well as a genuine concern about his welfare. *Damn,* she thought, *I wish I would have made a Bloody Mary and brought it upstairs with me.* To break the silence, she said, "Gabe, are you still there?"

"Yes, Sylvia, I'm still here. You know, Zane is a big boy. He probably just had one too many at Tim's Bar and Grill on the river and is still sleeping it off in his car somewhere."

"No, Gabe. I just feel that he's in trouble—that something dreadful happened to him. He just wouldn't do this. He wouldn't abandon me and the kids."

Sensing her desperation, Gabe replied, "Okay, Silva, there isn't a lot we can do at this point, but I'm not too busy right now, so I'll stop by your house on my way home, and we can talk."

"Thank you, Gabe. Thank you very much. I'll be waiting for your visit."

3

Denise Potts got out of her Ford Galaxy convertible at Diane Smith's apartment. She slowly walked up the sidewalk to the steps leading up to the small side porch. The June sun was beating down on her. It was a perfect morning. Denise climbed the steps to Diane's apartment and rang the doorbell. She stood there for a few moments, and when no one answered, she decided to just leave and have breakfast at the Maple Diner. As Denise turned to leave, she hesitated, turned back to the door, and decided to try one more time. After all, what if it had been a long night and they were both sleeping? She rang the bell again and then tried the door. To her surprise, the door gave way and opened.

Denise remained motionless and then said, "What the hell—tennis is tennis." She pushed the door open and yelled, "Di!" It was then that she saw Zane's corpse and the blood. She tried to scream, but no sound came out. She became weak in the knees, pivoting to escape the charnel house. She grabbed the porch railing and vomited and then slowly dropped to her knees as she tried to process the grizzly scene. The body had to be that of Zane Winston, although it was lying facedown on the stairs and she could not see the face. But it just had to be, she thought—his car, their affair. She then remembered Diane. "Oh my God!" Denise said. She turned to negotiate the steps to the apartment but could not go in. "The police, must call the police," she mumbled as she ran down to the sidewalk.

Once she was on the sidewalk, she stopped. She didn't know where to find a telephone. Denise did not know this neighborhood, and Diane had never mentioned any of the neighbors by name. Denise looked to the large, rather ornate house sitting to the east of Diane's apartment. It was the house of one of Putnam Landing's notable citizens, a local pottery magnet. He had been dead for many years, but his widow lived in the palatial home along with her housekeeper and other help. There was a carport held up by two ornate columns, and a door from the carport led down into the house. She ran for that door and began pounding on it. A rather pretty, tall, matronly woman opened the door and said, "May I help you?"

"Ma'am, please! You have to help me! I need a telephone! There's been a murder! There's a dead man! Blood everywhere! It's awful! Call the police!"

Ms. Evelyn Snead was an imposing woman wearing a black dress with large lavender flowers. Her graying hair pulled tightly back into a bun highlighted the depth of her dark eyes and high cheekbones. Ms. Snead wore the same basic black shoes that Denise's grandmother had worn. *Good God,* Denise thought, *this is 1956, isn't it?* Ms. Snead hailed from Upstate New York but had worked for the Rozanes for thirty years as a housekeeper and managing the day-to-day operations of the house and its servants. *Why am I thinking about this woman's clothes? There's a dead man.* "Please, ma'am! I need a phone. He's lying right inside the door on the steps! He's dead! You have to let me use the phone!"

Ms. Snead looked Denise up and down and with a disapproving look said, "You mean over there where that strumpet lives?"

"Ma'am, she's a friend of mine. Now let me use the damn phone!"

With that, Ms. Snead grudgingly moved to the side, allowing Denise entrance into the large house. She directed Denise to a telephone in the back of the reception hall. Denise picked up the receiver and dialed zero. An operator responded immediately. "Please!" Denise said. "Send the police to 947 Maple Place. There has been a murder!"

Gabriel St. John had been at the Winston residence for approximately an hour, trying to console Sylvia Winston, who by this time had become inebriated. She was ranting about Zane and his affairs on the one hand, and on the other crying that he could be lying somewhere hurt, all the while drinking gin and tonics and becoming drunker. The children were in and out of the room, wondering what a real policeman was doing in their home and asking if this had something to do with their father.

Sylvia had enough. She stood up with some difficulty and screamed, "If you two don't stay out of here, I'm going to beat you with a club!" her words slurring together. She then began to sob as the children left the room.

As she began to fall, Gabe rose from his chair and ran to catch her in his powerful arms. He eased her back down on to the couch, saying, "Sylvia, you have to calm down for the children's sake. We don't know that there's anything at all wrong with Zane, and your kids need to be reassured."

"How the hell can I reassure anyone in my state?"

"You can start by laying off the damn booze," Gabe quickly retorted.

"Oh, Gabe, he's probably with one of his whores."

Before he could respond to her, she had turned and kissed him. He could feel her full, soft lips on his. He remembered their times together. He responded to her as though they had never been apart. He could feel the yearning for her rising in his groin.

"Oh, Gabe, was I good? Am I still good? Why can't we, why can't we just—"

The telephone rang.

"I'm not answering it," she said.

Gabe, trying to compose himself, said, "But, Sylvia, it might be Zane."

With that, she rose from the coach and padded across the room to the telephone. "Hello," she said.

"Is this the Winston residence?" the voice on the other end of the line said.

"Yes—yes, it is," Sylvia replied.

"This is Lieutenant George from the Putnam Landing Police Department. Is Detective St. John there?"

"Yes, he is. I'll get him for you. It's a Lieutenant George from the police department. He wants you."

Gabe got up and walked to the phone. Sylvia smiled as she glanced at the obvious bulge in his pants. As she passed the phone to him, he said, "St. John. How can I help you?"

"Gabe, this is Roy George. We have a report of a murder at 947 Maple Place. You should get there now. There's a patrolman responding, but I need you there."

"Okay, Lieutenant. I'm on my way." He hung the phone up and said, "Sylvia, I have to go. I want you to stop drinking and talk with your kids about this."

She moved against him and said, "I know you still want me. I could see that when you got up off the couch."

"Sylvia, we can't do this. I have to go."

Detective St. John drove past the stone pillars that marked the entrance to Northridge, the area where Sylvia and Zane lived. He turned on the siren and sped around the traffic on Sycamore Avenue. He was thinking murder—murder in Putnam Landing. Violent crime was a rarity in this city of twenty-eight thousand people. It happened, but not often. He sped west until he arrived at the address. There was a patrol car out front with its lights flashing.

After parking in front of the house, he jumped out of his car and ran up to the house. He tried the front door, but it was locked. St. John was at the downstairs apartment, which was empty. Gabriel ran down the steps to the sidewalk and followed it around the left side of the house, where he saw the officer and a young woman on the small porch. He quickly ran around to the steps and climbed them. "Hi, Ed. What do we have?"

Ed Johnson was a two-year member of the Putnam Landing Police, still a rookie but with the makings of a good cop. "Two bodies, both shot.

The man is on the steps, and I think it's Zane Winston. The woman is upstairs on the bed, and I'm not sure who she is."

"Zane Winston? Are you sure?"

The patrolman responded, "I checked his wallet, and it is Zane Winston. He's been shot in the head, and most of it is gone. Go and look for yourself."

Gabe opened the door into the stairway. "God, what a mess," he said. As he rolled the body over, he said, "Jesus, it is Zane." There was an entrance wound about the size of a quarter just above the left eye, but at least half the back of the head was blown away. Blood, bone, and brain matter were scattered everywhere. It was common knowledge in Putnam Landing that Zane wore a large diamond pinky ring, and the ring was there. Gabe proceeded up the steps into the apartment. In the bedroom, he found Diane Smith's naked body sprawled on the bed. As he carefully rolled the body over, he saw only one exit wound about the size of a half dollar. *That means there's still a round in her body. Maybe there is hope for ballistics.*

Gabe returned to the porch and said to Ed, "Let's get the coroner here." He then turned to Denise. "Who are you, and what are you doing here?"

At seven thirty in the evening, the Lake Central airline arrived at the Dulles International Airport in Washington, DC. The two assassins rose from their seats and waited their turn to enter the aisle. As they exited, an attractive stewardess with a painted-on smile thanked them for flying Lake Central and said she hoped they would use the airline again.

Thomas Atherton and Carl Waters hit the tarmac and entered the terminal building. They were just about to go to the baggage claim when they were stopped by a tall thin man dressed in a black suit and white shirt. "Berger," Thomas said, "what in the hell are you doing here?"

Hans Berger, a German national and former SS officer, who had been helped into the country at the end of the war, as so many other scientists, engineers, teachers, and professionals had been, was the agency directive aid. They were former Nazis and SS officers, and Thomas Atherton did not completely trust any of them.

"The colonel wishes to see you immediately," Berger informed them through a thick accent.

"Immediately," Atherton responded. "Christ, we've had a long day. We were hoping for a shower and relaxation before the debriefing."

"You must meet with the colonel at once," Berger said. "He awaits you at his house."

"All right, all right, Hans. Tell him we'll be there, but we have to get our luggage and car."

Thomas and Carl jostled and pushed with the rest of the passengers to get to the baggage carousel. Two small overnight satchels were all they had, but it was a long process. The two men then walked to the lot where Thomas's car was parked. At long last, they located it, a 1955 D-type Jaguar in British racing green. The two assassins climbed into the aromas of leather, romance, and history. Thomas turned the key, and the Jag rumbled to life. By the time they arrived at the colonel's Georgetown brownstone, it was approaching nine o'clock. The traffic in Washington since the war had been unbearable.

The colonel was Colonel Benjamin Corbin, West Point and US Army. He was an imposing man at six feet two and 215 pounds, with a thick shock of white hair. He had the deep voice of authority to go with his demeanor. The colonel chain-smoked Camel cigarettes and enjoyed an occasional Cuban cigar. He had been an aide-de-camp to William J. "Wild Bill" Donovan, the spymaster who was the founder of modern American intelligence and who had created the OSS during the war. He had been assigned to Switzerland for the war, directing the OSS operations throughout much of Europe, and later, at the war's end, he was about to be sent to Japan.

When the war ended, Corbin was a natural for the newly formed CIA in 1947. He readily accepted the offer to become an analyst with the new agency, specializing on the European desk. He carried his military rank with him. By 1951, the colonel was bored silly. There was no adrenaline rush associated with writing analyses and papers on the East German Stasi and military. He never got to see or, more importantly, control the ultimate result of his efforts. In fact, he never knew what happened most of the time.

Corbin saw the need for a small, tightly controlled unit within the agency to provide deep cover infiltration and assassinations when necessary. In 1952, the colonel wrote a proposal delineating his thoughts and presented it to the director. In a matter of months, the proposal was accepted, and Corbin became the head of the special unit. He was given carte blanche approval to select the people on the team, and he relied heavily on recruiting the former OSS agents he had known and worked with during the war, men such as Carl Waters, who had developed a killer's instinct while serving with Patton in North Africa. The colonel and the OSS merely honed and refined those skills to kill Germans more efficiently and win the war.

Thomas Atherton was an exception to this practice. Atherton had been attending Cornell University until he enlisted in the spring of '44. He was commissioned to lieutenant in the Army Intelligence and stationed in Washington, DC. When the war ended in August 1945, this allowed him to return to Cornell to finish his BA in political science and a master's degree in international relations.

The day after his May 1952 graduation, his telephone rang, and the caller explained in a thick German accent that he was in the position to offer him a job. "If you are interested," the caller went on, "a car will be dispatched to your apartment at ten o'clock in the morning to transport you to the interview."

"What—what are you talking about? Who are you, and who do you represent?"

"I am sorry, Mr. Atherton. I can divulge no more information to you. If you are interested in working for good pay and good benefits, please confirm these arrangements. Otherwise, you will never hear from us again."

Atherton was intrigued by the mysterious phone call. He lit a Chesterfield, inhaled deeply, and replied, "Okay, okay. You send the car at ten o'clock in the morning, and I will be ready."

"Thank you, Mr. Atherton. We will see you in the morning." The line went dead.

Damn Kraut. The job is probably working for Adenauer at the German embassy.

The next morning, the car was prompt, and Atherton was driven to Colonel Corbin's home in Georgetown. Following introductions and small talk, the colonel explained to Atherton that he had known his father.

"My dad? How did you know him?"

"Your father's stamping plant in Vermont was awarded a military contract to produce the single-shot .45-caliber pistols that were issued to OSS agents during the war. In fact, he was in Zurich to meet with me when he tragically died."

"He was meeting with you?" Atherton asked.

"Yes, we had problems with the contract, and he came to Zurich to meet me."

Thomas Atherton Sr. had fallen, been pushed, or jumped from his hotel window. The circumstances surrounding his death were never verified. The Atherton family, Thomas Jr. and his two sisters and their mother, never knew what had happened to Thomas Sr.

"Mr. Atherton, I apologize, but we must move on."

"Yes, yes, of course, Colonel, please."

"Mr. Atherton, Thomas, I have a very special task force within a larger agency. I have been reviewing your military records, and I see that you are a qualified marksman with the .45, and your psychological profile appears to mesh with the needs of my task force."

"What are you saying, Colonel? That I'm a psychopath who would fit right in with the new CIA?"

The colonel had to choose his words carefully. While the army tests had shown a certain proclivity toward psychopathy, he could also function quite normally in society. The colonel needed the psychopathic portion of Atherton's psyche. "Well, my boy, it is more of a proclivity for individual work, such as infiltration and deep cover. You will be paid well. You will travel, and the benefits are great."

Atherton lit a Chesterfield. Though the whole thing sounded crazy, he was drawn in. "Okay, Colonel, where do I sign?"

"Hans!" the colonel yelled. The door to the large study opened, and a tall thin man dressed in a dark suit entered.

"Yah, Colonel," he responded.

The Kraut, Thomas thought.

"Take Mr. Atherton to your office to complete the paperwork for hire."

It all happened that quickly. Atherton thought, *This guy knew my dad. Maybe he was one of the last people to see him alive. I have to join this task force. I have to know.* Plus, the work sounded interesting.

As Atherton and Waters were exiting the Jag, Thomas said, "It looks like it could rain. Roll your window up, Carl. God knows how long we'll be in here."

"Yeah, I got it," Carl responded.

They climbed the sandstone steps leading up to the portico of the brownstone, and before they could ring the doorbell, the door swung open. Hans greeted them by saying, "He is waiting for you in the study." Without saying another word, he led the way down the wide hall to the study door at the foot of the stairway. Hans opened the study door, announced the two men, and disappeared into the depths of the room so as not to be seen.

The room was large and well appointed with wall-to-wall bookcases and period furniture. Two large windows faced the street where they had just parked. At this time of day, the study was dark. *That's the problem with these brownstones*, Atherton thought. *They're built right next to each other, and there's no natural light. They're depressingly dark.*

The colonel was seated in a green-leather swivel chair behind a large desk. If Thomas had to guess, he would say it was an original Chippendale dating from about 1750 to 1770. Covering the wide oak flooring were area oriental rugs in various states of wear, from what he could tell in the dim light. On the desk was a double student lamp with green glass shades. Between the two front windows was a marble-top stand with a Victorian wrought iron lamp. Directly across from the door they had just entered was a Sheridan two-drawer stand with a lamp, also with a green glass shade.

"Come in, gentlemen. Come in," the colonel belted out with his deep voice. He rose from his chair and motioned for the two men to sit in the pair of wing chairs angled in front of his desk. *Again, Chippendale,* Atherton thought. "Can I offer you a drink, perhaps a bourbon or a brandy?"

Atherton did not drink, and Carl, while he did, did not care for either of the offerings and replied, "I'll take a beer."

"Ah, regretfully, Carl, I do not have any beer at this time."

"That's okay, Colonel. Let's just move on," Carl replied. "Fill me in on your mission."

"I'm Denise Potts, a friend of Diane Smith's. I'm afraid that something awful has happened to her."

"Did you find the bodies?" Gabe asked.

"Bodies? Did you say *bodies,* Detective?"

"Yes, I'm afraid I did. Ms. Smith's body is up in her bedroom. What were you doing here, Ms. Potts?"

"Diane and I had a tennis match at nine thirty this morning, and I was here to pick her up."

The detective retrieved a pack of cigarettes from his pocket and offered one. She gratefully accepted his offer. She said, "Thanks," as Gabe lit her cigarette with his Zippo.

"Now tell me," the detective said, "exactly what you did when you arrived here."

"Well, I pulled up beside the Cadillac and thought, *Oh boy, what am I in for? Did he spend the night? Did he just stop by this morning?*" She took a long draw on the Chesterfield and felt it bite her lungs, as well as its calming effect. "I went up the sidewalk to the steps, up to this porch."

"Excuse me," the detective interjected, "but when you say *he,* who do you mean?"

Denise exhaled and responded, "Why, Zane Winston, Diane's boss at Winston Optics."

"How did you know that it was Zane Winston at Diane's apartment?"

"Well, Jesus, Detective, it's a well-known secret that they've been having an affair and his car was parked in the driveway."

"Please, proceed, Ms. Potts," Gabe gently urged.

"Okay, well, I rang the bell, but there was no response, so I knocked on the door, and when I did, it opened. I called for Diane, and again, no answer. I opened the door a little farther and went into the stairwell, where I found a body and a bloody mess. I returned to the porch, where I almost passed out, but then I realized that I must call the authorities. I went next door"—she gestured toward the Rozane house—"and called the police."

Gabe glanced over at the house and then turned back to Denise. As he looked at her, he thought, *A very attractive woman*, so he asked, "What was your relationship to Zane Winston?"

"What?" Denise indignantly responded. "Just what do you mean, *my relationship*, Detective?"

"Just that, Ms. Potts. How well did you know Zane Winston?"

"Not that well, Detective. Look, if you're attempting to tie me in any way to what's happened here, you're barking up the wrong tree. I met Zane Winston only once. I was leaving Diane's apartment, and he was arriving. We ironically met on the same stairway in passing. That's it! One time only. That's it."

"That's the only time you met him?" St. John said.

"Yes," Denise responded. "I knew him vicariously through Diane. I mean, well, their relationship and only what she told me, but that's it, and she never shared too many details, and only now and then did she reveal anything about their private lives together. I never asked or pried into their relationship."

"All right, Ms. Potts, I'm going to have to ask you to come down to the station and give your formal statement. Would ten o'clock tomorrow morning be convenient for you?"

"Yes, Detective St. John, I'll be there."

"Thank you, Ms. Potts. You may now leave."

As Denise was getting into her car, she noticed two police cars stopping in front, along with an ambulance. A car also pulled up behind hers from the alley. She carefully backed out into the alley and proceeded home.

The car arriving was Dr. Elijah Mason, a semiretired physician who was the elected county coroner. Dr. Mason had practiced in Chicago in the 1930s after graduating from medical school at the University of Illinois. He had seen his fill of gangland shootings and murders before being drafted in to the Army Medical Corps, where he served in a medical unit in France. Following the war, he decided to return to his family home in Putnam Landing. He was a bachelor who enjoyed a quiet life in the old family home on the Elk Eye River. Not too much was required of a coroner in Putnam Landing. An occasional sudden death of an older resident simply required that he certify a natural death and return home. Dr. Eli, as he was known, maintained a practice where he saw just a few patients two days a week. He had a nurse, Ms. Betty Shaw, who helped him with patient care and record keeping. Dr. Mason lived a relatively easy life on the bank of the Elk Eye.

As he walked up the stairs, he encountered Gabriel St. John on the porch. "Gabe, how are you doing? What do we have here?"

"Hi, Eli. Two bodies, gunshot wounds. The one in the stairwell is Zane Winston, and the other one is a female on the bed in the bedroom."

"Zane?" Dr. Eli replied. "Oh no. My goodness, a jealous husband?"

"Don't know, Eli. I want you to tell me," Gabe retorted.

"Okay, Gabe. Let me get to it." With that, the coroner entered the stairwell to begin his work. He first observed the position of Zane's body and made notes. He then put on gloves and lifted his body to examine the entrance wounds. He rolled the body back over to examine the exit wounds. "Hum," he muttered as he glanced to the top of the stairs. Dr. Mason peeled off the gloves and made some more notes and drawings in the small notebook.

While he was writing, Gabe joined him. "Well, what do you think, Eli?"

The coroner finished writing and said, "Let's see the other one." Gabe led the way up the steps, then through the living room back to the bedroom. "Oh, I know her," the coroner said. "I treated her for a yeast infection several months ago. I guess I can tell you that now, as it might help the case. I'm not sure I recall the name. Betty will know, but I think it's Smith. Yes, Diane Smith, that's it. It was last winter that she came to the office, a beautiful young woman, as you can see. Too bad, too bad. Well, let me examine her."

As Dr. Mason was pulling on another set of gloves, Gabe walked out into the living room where three patrolmen were looking around. "Hey, you guys, I want you to go house to house and see if any of the neighbors saw or heard anything."

One of the boys in blue responded with, "Okay, Sarge, we'll get right to it."

With that, the patrolmen began descending the stairs, and Gabe rejoined Dr. Mason in the bedroom. The coroner was busy making notes and drawings when Gabe asked, "What do you think, Dr. Eli?"

Dr. Eli looked up from his notepad over the glasses perched on the end of his nose. "This was no jealous husband or lover. This was a professional hit. I've seen it too many times back in Chicago, one round in the trunk to disable the mark and one in the head to finish them off."

"Jesus Christ, Eli, are you telling me this is a mob hit?"

"No, no. I'm not saying who did it. That's your job to figure out. I am merely saying that, in my opinion, this is a professional hit. I've seen these wounds in Chicago since the thirties, but I also saw them in Europe toward the end of the war. I don't know who or why, but these are professional hits."

"But look at her; she's shot three in the chest."

"You're right," Dr. Eli replied, "but did you notice the pistol in her right hand, a .32 ACP Walther PP, a common weapon of the Waffen SS and other German officers. It has been fired once. The round must be in the back of the closet. I think there were at least two shooters, one in this closet and one probably in the closet in the living room. She was undressing for a shower or bath, whatever, she heard something in the closet, got her gun, the door opened, she fired and presumably missed (there's no blood), and he fired twice, killing her. A second man met Zane from the top of the stairs. He shot twice. Zane was dead before he hit the stairs. Without a doubt, they had silencers on their weapons to avoid alerting their neighbors."

"But, Eli, what about her gun?" Gabe asked. "Wouldn't her shot have alerted someone?"

"Well, who's to say? A 7.65 mm pistol going off in a second-story apartment would very likely sound like a kid's cap gun or a small firecracker down on the street. Maybe no one even heard it or gave it any notice if they did hear something. I would say the time of death for both of them is between five and seven last night. I'll know more after the autopsies, but I wouldn't count on too much more if I were you. You've got your work cut out for you. Good luck, my boy." As Dr. Mason was exiting the apartment, the bodies were bagged for removal to the morgue.

The detective lit a cigarette and began a thorough search of the dead woman's apartment. He began in the bedroom closet, where a patrolman was diligently digging out the bullet from Diane Smith's pistol. "Sir," the officer said, "this is tough going at it with just this penknife."

"Keep at it. We need that slug for ballistics. We need to see if it has any traces of blood on it."

"Okay, sir. I'll get it out, but it may not be in very good shape when I do."

"Just do your best." Removing the shoes from the closet floor was a task unto itself. There were twenty-two pairs of stiletto heels in various colors, some flats, sandals, and tennis shoes, all size 9. He made an entry into his notebook as to each pair, the size and color. "Good god, this woman had enough shoes to open a department store," Gabriel said.

He then completed the inventory of the dresses, suits, slacks, jackets, and blouses the patrolman had removed from the closet and piled neatly onto the floor so he could get to the bullet hole in the back of the closet. The cop had taken the dressing table bench into the closet to stand on while he dug at the bullet. As he shifted his weight more to the right side, the bench dropped down into the floor, throwing the officer off and onto the floor.

"Shit!" the cop yelled. "What the hell happened?"

At the commotion, Gabe, who had been going through the chest of drawers, hurried to the closet. "What's wrong? What's going on, Officer?"

"Well, damned if I know, sir," the cop replied as he untangled himself from the closet floor. "The legs of the bench must have broken," he said as he exited the mayhem of the closet.

"Are you all right?" Gabe asked as he glanced at the cop's name on his uniform pocket, Goodmore.

"I think so, sir. I shifted my weight to the right side of the bench, and it gave way, throwing me into the wall and on to the right side. When I hit the wall, I fell down to the floor."

"Okay, Goodmore," the detective said as he crawled into the closet to retrieve the bench. When he lifted the bench, he noticed that the legs were intact. They hadn't broken. They had sunk into the closet floor. A loose board had given way, and the legs had dropped into the space. *What the hell?* Gabe thought as he peered into the dark crevice in the closet floor. "Hey, Goodmore, do you have a flashlight?"

"It's in my patrol car, sir."

Just then, another voice said, "I've got mine. Do you need it?" The three officers who had been canvassing the neighborhood had returned and were in the living room waiting for the detective to debrief them. When they heard the loud noise in the bedroom, they had hurried there.

"Yes, I do."

The patrolman passed his flashlight into the closet, and Gabe grabbed it from him. He turned it on and pointed it into the void of the closet floor. "What the hell is this?"

As Gabe was reaching into the hole in the closet floor, a loud voice interrupted him. "Where's Sergeant St. John?" The voice belonged to Lieutenant George, who had left the station to make an appearance at this high-level crime scene.

Gabe yelled, "Here, Lieutenant, in here. I think you better see this." With that, the detective extracted a device from the hole. "It's kind of heavy," Gabe warned him as he handed it out to Lieutenant George.

"My God, what is this thing, Gabe?"

"I think it's a radio or some type of communication equipment. Wait a minute. There's something else in here." Gabe reached in and pulled out another small automatic pistol in a leather holster, along with a box of ammunition. He crawled out of the closet and stood up.

Lieutenant George was examining the find from the closet. "It is a radio. It is a damned radio. Who was this woman and why did she have a radio and two guns? For Christ's sake, this is Putnam Landing, not New York City."

Gabe began examining the radio and the pistol. "This is a Russian Soviet radio, and the pistol is a 7.65 mm Czech CZ 50 with German, probably East German, markings."

"What!" George exclaimed. "What are you telling me, Gabe? Are you saying that these two were some kind of agents or spies?"

"No, Lieutenant George, what I'm saying is that the radio is a wartime leftover. It's available on the surplus market, but this pistol is a different story. This automatic is issued to the East German Stasi agents. I don't know a lot about this, but I read that this CZ is the current issue to the East German Stasi. It's a 7.65 mm 32 ACP. In our jargon, a small caliber, but it hits like the kick from a mule. Our government would not import this pistol, and if anyone could obtain one, the chances are one in a million that it would be marked in this way."

The lieutenant was trying to absorb all of this and lamented, "Oh God, what do we do?"

"Well, sir," Gabe said, "I strongly suggest that you call the FBI. Also, I strongly suggest that this information not leave this room. Do you four understand?" Gabe looked at the patrolmen in the bedroom. "I'm serious, men. You have got to keep quiet. This may have national security implications. No talking."

"Yes, sir," the room full of officers replied.

"And no interviews or talking to the *Democrat*." The *Democrat* was the Putnam Landing newspaper. "Only the Lieutenant will talk to them. Is that understood?" They nodded. "Okay," Gabe said, looking at the four officers, "take this stuff to the station, talk to no one, say nothing, and put them in the lieutenant's office on his desk. Leave the office, close the door, and say nothing. Do you understand?"

"Yes, sir, we do." One of the patrolmen picked up the radio; another the pistol and the box of ammunition.

"Hey, I also want to talk with each of you at ten o'clock in the morning."

"But, sir," one of the cops responded, "it's Sunday, and I'm off tomorrow."

"It's Sunday, and you be at the station at ten o'clock. Is that clear?"

"Yes, okay, sir. I'll be there."

"Good," Gabriel responded. "I'll see you then."

When the four cops had left, Lieutenant Roy George was still trying to process the whole scene. "Jesus, Gabe, what do we have here?"

"I don't know. I mean, maybe nothing, but that's why I think we should get some help. We need some help, some outside help. I think you should notify the FBI."

"Yes," Roy replied, "you're right, and I need to talk with Chief Cochran as soon as I can."

"And I need to talk with Sylvia Winston. It's already one o'clock, and I just pray that she hasn't already heard."

"Right, you go console the widow, and I'll head back to the station."

The two men exited the apartment, sealing it with yellow tape. The two had their missions.

The rain had stopped by the time the two assassins left Colonel Corbin's brownstone. They had related to the colonel the events of their mission. He had listened intently before asking, "What about the Ruskie?"

"Who, the Russian?"

"The Russian physicist," Corbin said. "He was supposed to be with the other two."

"He wasn't, Colonel," Atherton stated. "It was just the two of them, no one else."

The colonel raised his voice. "Well, goddamn it, he was supposed to be with them. Our agent in the Hungarian delegation told us that he was going to her apartment with that Zane, that weak son of a bitch owner of the Optical Factory."

"Colonel, I don't know what to say. He wasn't with them. We took care of the other two and got the hell out of there."

The colonel, looking grave, said, "The contract called for three. You hit two. There is one left. You must get him. We suspect very strongly that he was working for the woman to get the design for the gyroscope out of the country. We know that he is from the Ukraine. We know that he defected to the Germans in the face of Operation Barbarossa in '42. We know that the Kraut put him to work at Peenemünde working on the V1 and V2 projects. We know that the Russians want him back or dead. Now, gentlemen, this is what we know. I am willing to bet you that Dr. Victor Marchenko is scared shitless and is right now trying frantically to get out of the country."

"We will take care of him, Colonel," Atherton assured him, "but first it's home and a hot shower, several bourbons, and some R&R. Send me his dossier and whatever other information you have on him, and Carl and I will go over it. We'll formulate a plan."

Colonel Corbin, who would rather have had them on a return flight to Ohio, shrugged. "All right. I will send it by agency courier."

As the two were driving home, Carl said, "I think we fucked up, and I think he's pissed."

Gabriel St. John got into his car, lit a cigarette, and backed down into the alley behind Diane Smith's apartment. He negotiated the side streets until he arrived at Sycamore Avenue, a main north-south street in Putnam Landing. He turned north and once again headed for Sylvia Winston's house. He knew full well she had been drinking heavily since he left her this morning, and he knew this was not going to be an easy task. As he approached the stone pillars on each side of the entrance to Northridge Circle, where Zane and Sylvia lived, he tossed his cigarette out the window and slowly drove down the residential street to the house. Detective St. John approached the door and rang the bell.

Brad answered the door, saying, "Can I help you?"

"Hello, Brad. Do you remember me from this morning?"

"Yes, sir, I do. You're the policeman."

"Very good, Brad. Is your mother here?"

"Yes. She's in the living room on the sofa."

"Thank you, young man. I will just show myself in. Where is your sister, Caroline?"

"Upstairs in my room. We're playing fort, and she's the enemy."

"Okay, good," the detective replied. "Now, will you please go back upstairs and finish the war while I go and talk with your mother?"

Brad said, "Well, okay, but Mom is really sound asleep, and she has been there most of the day."

Gabe, in his most detective and serious voice, stated, "I really must speak with your mother. Please go back upstairs and stay with Caroline in the bedroom until I call you."

"Okay, Officer, I'll do that. Is this about our daddy?"

Gabe felt a pang of hurt welling up in his gut as he said, "We'll talk to you in a little while. Please stay in your room, both of you."

"Yes, sir, I will, and I'll keep Caroline with me."

"Thanks, Brad. Now please go."

As the child scampered off, the detective entered the living room through the hall door. He discovered Sylvia passed out on the couch, an empty glass tipped over on the floor beside her. She had not gotten dressed, and the silk robe she was wearing was slightly parted, revealing her right breast and a patch of raven-black hair between her thighs. Her full lips were opened just a little. They were moist. Gabe had a flashback of their times together, of those lips kissing him, engulfing him. He shook his head. *Whoa, no, no,* he thought. *I can't think these things.* He reached down and gently placed the robe over her, picked up the empty glass, and found his way to the kitchen. He located the coffeepot, found the coffee, and proceeded to make a pot of strong black brew.

He was going to have to ask Sylvia uncomfortable questions about her whereabouts the previous night. *Could she have done it?* he thought. *Could she have been waiting somehow in Smith's apartment and as the jealous wife shot them both?* "No!" he said. "She's many things but not a murderer." Still, she had motive, and he had to question her in order to eliminate her as a suspect. That was going to be a chore.

Gabe sat down at the kitchen table. He lit a cigarette while waiting for the coffee to brew and began reminiscing about Zane Winston. He remembered him as a chubby seventh grader who had everything that he ever wanted, including the best clothes, the most expensive bike, and a chauffeur-driven Packard to take him to and from West View School. Zane was not a good student, and his grades reflected that, at least until sixth grade when he got As and Bs in every subject. Gabe remembered the teacher that year—Ms. Phillips, a young, beautiful woman who had been hired for her first teaching job in Putnam Landing. This was 1932, and nobody in Putnam Landing had too much of anything, and some people had nothing. Ms. Phillips, as he remembered, lived in a little cottage on Oakwood Avenue owned by Zane Winston Sr. Several nights a month, the chauffeur-driven Packard would be parked in front of the house, and by that Christmas, Ms. Phillips was driving a new Ford V8 Coupe. He remembered that she was mysteriously gone that April. As far as he knew, no one had ever heard of her again. *That's how it works,* Gabe thought. *Zane gets As and Bs, the old man gets some on the side, Ms. Phillips gets a house, car, money, and maybe a kid, and the rest of us are left to struggle.* That was until President Roosevelt took office and pulled the country out of the Depression. Gabe couldn't remember much about Zane in the seventh grade at Roosevelt Junior High School. That was when they started changing classes, and Gabe had no classes with Zane. Then in eighth grade, Zane was gone to some fancy, expensive prep school on the East Coast. After he and Sylvia were married, Zane would not have anything to do with Gabe. Gabe chuckled. *Probably because he knew I was there before him.*

The coffeepot quit perking, and Gabe rose from the table and walked to the sink. He held his cigarette under the faucet and dropped it into the garbage can. He then proceeded to the cupboard where he found two large coffee mugs. After filling these with the hot brew, he carried them into the living room to wake up Sylvia. He placed the two mugs on the coffee table and knelt in front of her. Gabe gently nudged her and softly called her name. Sylvia turned her head to the back of the couch and continued sleeping. Gabe persisted in jostling her.

She opened her eyes and, turning toward him, said, "Oh, Gabe, it's you. You were in my dream, and here you are."

"Sylvia, you've got to wake up and sit up," Gabe responded as he put his arm under her back to help her sit up while trying to keep the flimsy robe around her.

When he had her in an upright position, she looked at him, her eyes wide open and her face pale. "My God, it's Zane, isn't it? You've found him, haven't you? Is he … is he all right? Is he hurt or in trouble?"

The detective picked up the mug of coffee and handed it to her. "Drink this, Sylvia. It will help to clear your head."

"I don't want Goddamn coffee! I need to know what you found out about Zane."

"Sylvia, drink some of this, and then we'll talk," Gabe calmly replied.

She gripped the mug and took a large swallow of the coffee. As she was swallowing it, she gestured toward the coffee table. Gabe retrieved the pack of Philip Morris cigarettes for her. "My God, Gabe, this coffee is strong. It's like drinking lye," she commented as she lit the cigarette. "Now tell me about my husband."

Gabe hesitated for a moment, but then in his most professional detective's voice, he said, "Sylvia, I regretfully inform you that your husband, Zane Winston, is dead. He was murdered sometime yesterday afternoon or early evening as best we can tell right now. We will know more after the autopsy."

Sylvia took a long, deep drag on her cigarette. She finished her coffee, all the while trying to process what the detective had just said. *Zane, Zane, dead, Zane murdered, autopsy, what in the hell,* she thought. *What the hell is he talking about?* She stubbed out the Philip Morris in the ashtray on the coffee table, looked at Gabe, and said, "What the hell do you mean, dead, murdered?"

"Sylvia, I am so sorry, but Zane was found dead around nine thirty this morning."

"Where!" she screamed. "Where? Some jealous husband? Some spurned lover?"

"We're not sure at this point. We just don't know yet. We're still working on it."

"Where did you find him?"

"He was in the apartment of a Diane Smith on Maple Place," Gabe replied.

"Diane Smith, that Goddamned whore. I knew he was doing her. I just knew it. Did she kill him?"

"No, Sylvia, she too was murdered," Gabe responded.

"What? What are you saying, Gabe? They were both killed?"

"Yes, Sylvia, both of them were shot, and we—"

"A jealous husband or boyfriend, without a doubt," she interjected.

Gabe reiterated, "We just don't know, Sylvia. It's too early in the investigation. We'll know more after the autopsies."

"*Autopsies?* Do you mean that he has to be cut up, mutilated?"

Gabe regretted using that term. "Sylvia," he calmly said, "the law requires it in the case of homicide. There's nothing I can do."

"But, Gabe," she murmured, "he'll be all cut up. How will the children know who they're looking at?"

"I'm sorry, Sylvia. It has to be done. We need to know who perpetrated this terrible crime and why." This was all Gabe could come up with in the moment, and he was hoping Sylvia would let it go. She did, at least momentarily.

Gabe was wondering where the tears were. He had expected a hysterical woman, but instead he saw a stone-cold, sober, calm, and rational Sylvia. As he started to question her, she said, "You know, Gabe, I can't cry. I mean, I know that I should, but the tears just won't come. I loved Zane—well, part of me did, as the father of my children and as a provider—but I don't think I ever really loved him in a passionate, deep sense. He was never faithful, not from the day we were married. He always had something on the side. I mean, the late nights, the missed dinners, the scent of one of his whores on him. My reaction was to drink more and spend more and to refuse him on those rare occasions that he wanted to make love. You know, I actually liked Diane even though I knew she was screwing my husband. Maybe the tears will come when I tell the children, but they're not here now."

At that moment, Brad and Caroline entered the living room, just as Gabe was thinking, *Wow, she's a strong woman. I've never seen this side of her.*

"Mom!" Brad said. "Caroline is supposed to be dead, but she refuses to die."

"Mom, it's not true," Caroline said. "He missed me, and I took the fort."

Sylvia, in her best, calm, loving voice, said, "Kids, I love you both so much, but you have to go back to your room and let me talk with the detective. I promise I will be upstairs to talk with both of you in just a little while, but you must leave now." With that, the children turned and exited the room.

"Sylvia," Gabe said, "you have to talk to them and tell them what has happened."

"I know that, and I will, but not right now. I'll do this in my own way and in my own time."

Gabe decided for himself that she had nothing to do with the murders. He said in a sympathetic voice, "They'll come, Sylvia, the tears. It could be that you've just steeled yourself for so long that the wall isn't down. When it does crack and crumble, so will you."

She stared at him for several seconds before replying, "Yes, well maybe, I don't know. I haven't looked at it that way. Thank you so much for being here with me. I'm just not sure that I would have had the strength to face this day except in a bottle. You've helped me so much." The detective sensed her vulnerabilities creeping back. He could see her face soften and her color returning to her cheeks. As she repositioned herself on the sofa, her flimsy gown opened.

It was time to leave. Gabe stood. He could see her creamy body where the gown was parted. Her soft breasts with their large nipples, the thick patch of dark pubic hair between her lovely thighs, he remembered it all. And as he stood looking at her and recalling their times together, he was becoming hard. He could feel his erection straining against his trousers. Gabe said, "I'll need you to come to the station in the morning at ..." Before he could finish his sentence, Sylvia had unzipped his fly and freed his cock from its restraints. She had her hand wrapped around it, and as Gabe was about to protest, she engulfed it with her mouth. "Oh my God, Sylvia," Gabe uttered. Just seconds before he exploded, he stopped her rhythmic movements and pushed her back on to the sofa. He parted her thighs and entered her with one thrust. He quickly came in a thunderous orgasm and remained inside her until he sensed her orgasm building. He pressed closer to her, and she entered into an earth-shattering orgasm of her own. Gabe was afraid that her vocalizations might bring the children downstairs, so he pulled out of her and stood up. Sylvia leaned forward and took Gabe's cock in her mouth, moving back and forth to drain the remaining drops of semen. When she released his penis, he quickly put it back in his pants and zipped his fly.

"Oh, sweet Jesus, Gabe, that was wonderful. That's the best sex I've had in years, and I mean that."

"Sylvia," Gabe quietly said, "do you realize what could happen to me if anyone ever found out about this?"

"Jesus, Gabe, do you think I would ever say a word about this to anybody? You should know me better than that. Of course, you didn't have a rubber, and you didn't pull out, so who knows. You put a load into me, and I might get pregnant, but I don't care. I'll have your child."

Oh shit, Gabe thought. *What have I done?* He was visibly flustered and tried to return to the professional detective. "I'll need you to come to the station at ten o'clock in the morning to give a statement."

"I'll be there, Gabe." She got up from the couch and kissed him deeply. He felt the familiar stirrings once again, but his time he was able to break away from her.

"Okay, Sylvia, I'll see you in the morning."

As he drove away, he lit a cigarette and thought, *What the hell have you done, Gabriel? You've not only put your job on the line, you've put your life on the line. You know how Sylvia is, especially when she's been drinking. She's liable to blab this all over town.* But it was good, he had to admit, just like old times.

Sunday morning arrived too soon for Thomas Atherton. He had spent Saturday evening with his female companion, Cheryl Griggs. They had spent the night drinking too much bourbon and having hard, passionate sex. Cheryl was twenty-eight and had moved to Washington, DC, right after graduating from high school in Ohio. She had met Atherton two years ago at a birthday party of a mutual friend. She fell madly in love with him the first night they spent together. Thomas dismissed her love as mere infatuation and would never discuss any future for them. He only wanted her available to him when he was home.

She had left her home in Ohio under questionable circumstances. Supposedly she'd had an affair with one of her teachers her senior year, resulting in a pregnancy. She left Ohio for Washington, DC, hoping to leave that part of her life behind her. Cheryl had gotten a job at the general accounting office, the GAO, as a clerk typist. She had worked hard and advanced to the position of clerk-typist supervisor with about thirty typists under her. Cheryl had tried to explain her life in Ohio to Thomas one night after they had made amazing love, but he would have none of it. He coldly cut her off, stating that it was the here and now that he cared about—nothing more. She never raised the subject again. Cheryl never asked Thomas where he worked or what he did. She never pried into his past or present life, from that evening on. Nevertheless, her loyalty to him never wavered.

It was six thirty in the morning when the doorbell to Atherton's apartment began ringing. He had been alerted as to someone in the corridor when he heard the heavy metal door at the end of the hall opening and closing from the stairway entrance. He sat straight up and grabbed the .38 from the bedside stand. He stood up and pulled on his bathrobe before proceeding to the window in the living room.

Peering down to the street, he saw a white 1955 Chevrolet with the familiar black-and-white government license plates. He relaxed and moved to answer the door, so as to stop the franticly ringing doorbell. When he opened the door, a fresh-faced kid asked, "Are you Mr. Thomas Atherton?"

"Yes," Atherton replied as he shielded half of his body behind the door, still holding the Model 10 in his right hand. "What can I do for you?"

"Sir, I'm Roger Bib, a courier from the agency. I have a delivery for you from Colonel Ben Corbin."

"Oh, Jesus Christ, at this time on a Sunday morning?"

"I'm sorry, sir, but I was told to get this to you ASAP."

"Okay, okay, kid. Give it to me." Atherton took the large manila envelope. He signed for it and closed the door. He glanced at the envelope stamped Top Secret Eyes Only, and then he opened the closet door and placed it on the shelf. He returned to the bedroom to arouse Cheryl, pausing at the foot of the bed to view her naked body. He watched her ample bosom rise and fall with each breath. *She's beautiful*, he thought, feeling the stirring of an erection. Atherton slid out of the bathrobe, letting it drop to the floor. He dropped the Smith & Wesson on top of the robe and crawled up the bed toward Cheryl's sleeping body. When he reached her knees, he gently parted them and buried his face between her thighs.

Cheryl murmured, "Oh my, what a nice way to wake up." She then convulsed into orgasm. Atherton was fully erect and was positioning himself to enter her when she stopped him. Cheryl slid down his body until she found his hard-on. She quickly took it into her mouth and began a rhythmic up-and-down administration until Atherton climaxed. She held him in her mouth until he went soft. Then with her soft, pouty lips tightly clinched, she squeezed his last few drops into her mouth and let his penis drop out. She got off the bed and said, "I'm going to shower. Breakfast is on you."

Thomas watched Cheryl disappear into the bathroom. He got up, pulled on his robe from the floor, replaced the .38 in the bedside table, and headed for the kitchen to cook breakfast. They feasted on bacon, eggs, toast, and a pot of strong black coffee. As they finished eating, Atherton lit a cigarette while having the last of the coffee. Cheryl, who had not bothered to dress after her shower, sat naked on the kitchen chair. "Are we going to do anything today or just stay around here?"

"I have work to do, so you're going to have to leave."

"Are you sure, Tom?" she questioned as she repositioned herself on the chair so that her vaginal lips were slightly parted as she sat facing him.

"Well, uh … well …" He thought, *We could always review that file tomorrow*, but then reality hit him—the colonel, the botched job. "Oh Christ, no, you've got to leave." With that, Cheryl got up from the chair and obediently went to the bedroom to begin dressing.

Atherton followed her. He sat on the bed watching her dress. She picked up her garter belt from the clothes scattered on the floor. She put it on and then found her hose. As she was fastening her garters to the hose, Atherton said, "Cheryl, we've been together for quite a while, and throughout our time together, we've never had any birth control. I've never worn a rubber. I hate the damn things, but I've never used one, and you've never gotten pregnant."

Cheryl continued dressing, putting on her panties a leg at time. She responded, "Well, I tried to tell you once about my past life, but you said you didn't want to hear about me getting pregnant my senior year, about having a baby that died, and about the doctor saying that I would probably never get pregnant again."

"Oh, okay, yeah, yeah, okay, I guess I remember. But, well, it's not 100 percent, is it?"

"Probably not, but don't worry yourself. If I get pregnant, I'll have your child and never burden you or tell anyone." She stepped into her black stilettos and moved toward the door into the hall. "Will you call me this week?"

"I will, Cheryl."

And with that, she exited the apartment, closing the door behind her.

When Atherton was satisfied that she was gone, he retrieved the package from the living room closet. He returned to the bedroom, where he tossed it on the bed as he reached for the bedside telephone. After dialing Carl's telephone number, he listened to the endless ringing. "Damn!" he said. "He's probably still with that whore of his. Oh well, not any different from me." He hung up. Thomas proceeded into the bathroom for a shower. *I'll call him when I'm finished,* he thought as he turned on the water for the shower.

Detective St. John had spent a long night in bed, though one short of sleep. He could not get his encounter with Sylvia Winston out of his head. This against the backdrop of a double murder caused him to toss and turn most of the night. When Gabe wasn't tossing and turning, he was sitting at the kitchen table drinking shots of bourbon and smoking. Finally, at four thirty, he drifted off into a light sleep. He opened his eyes at seven thirty and said, "To hell with this." He got out of bed, showered, dressed, and set off to Kate's Diner for coffee before going to the station.

It was 9:40 a.m. when Gabe walked into the station. The quick cup of coffee at Kate's turned into a full breakfast. Kate had read about the murders in the Sunday *Democrat* and would have none of "just coffee" for Gabe.

As he neared the station door, he caught sight of Denise Potts sitting on the bench in the waiting area. She was dressed in a short white skirt and a green blouse with black high heels. Gabe had a glimpse of a white triangle as her legs slightly parted when she stood up. "Detective St. John," she said as she approached him, "I'm here to give my statement."

"Yes, Ms. Potts. Give me a few minutes, and I'll be right with you."

At that moment, the station door swung open, and the grieving widow entered the waiting area. "Hi, Gabe, I'm here at 10:00 a.m.

as requested. I'm ready to tell all, anything you want to know." She approached Gabe, stopping just in front of him.

Gabe took a step back but not before catching a whiff of her breath. *Good God,* he thought, *she's been on the bottle, and it's not even ten o'clock.* "Oh, Sylvia, whoa, good morning. Have a seat, and I'll be with you in a few minutes. Oh, by the way, Sylvia, this is Denise Potts. Ms. Potts is the one who discovered the bodies and called us."

Sylvia, looking Denise up and down, was about to speak when Denise said, "I am so sorry for your loss, Mrs. Winston. Diane was my friend, and this whole thing is just, well, it's just terrible."

"Thank you, Ms. Potts," Sylvia responded as Gabe gently took her elbow and led her to a chair away from Denise. As he placed her in the chair, she whispered, "I'm not wearing underwear."

Gabe quickly straightened up and stepped back, saying, "I'll be with you ladies in a few minutes. If you would like a cup of coffee, I can get it for you."

Both refused the offer, and Gabe opened the glass door into the large detective room. Once inside, he found the lieutenant in his office, still puzzling over the contents of Diane Smith's closet. The radio and the holstered automatic pistol were on his desk. "Gabe, who the hell was this woman, and what was she doing here in Putnam Landing?"

"Roy, I can't figure it out. She might have been a spy of some sort, but why here? I was awake half the night trying to put it together. And if she was a spy, for whom was she spying, and what was Zane's connection? Was she just his latest piece of tail or was there another connection? What they have in common is the Optics Factory. Wasn't there some Eastern European delegation or group visiting the factory this week?"

Roy George said, "Yes. They were Hungarians. They stayed at the Clairton Hotel while visiting Zane's company. I think we better find out what's going on at that factory. What are they up to? What are they making—and for whom? You know, during the war, Winston had secret contracts."

"So," Gabe said, "could some of those have carried over?"

The lieutenant, sensing an early lead in the case, said, "I don't know, but I think we had better find out what's going on there."

"Okay, Roy. I'll get on that the first thing in the morning, but right now I have two interviews to do." He began leaving Roy's office.

"Gabe," the lieutenant yelled, "I'm calling the FBI first thing Monday morning."

Gabe found a room for the interviews and called for Denise Potts. When Betty, the receptionist, showed Denise into the interview room, Gabe could not help but notice her compact little body. *Jesus*, he thought, *I have work to do.*

Denise positioned herself on the wooden chair, being mindful of keeping her knees together so as not to show the Detective too much. The interview was routine. It was a rehash of her statement from the previous day at Diane Smith's apartment, except more formal, as it was written and signed by Denise.

As Denise was walking out of the room, he said, "Ms. Potts, I may have to contact you again, so if you leave town, please leave a phone number of how you can be reached."

"Oh, don't worry, Detective. I'm not going anywhere until September, and I would like to hear from you."

"Thank you, Ms. Potts. I'll keep that in mind," Gabe responded as he watched her exit the room. He sat back in the chair and lit a Chesterfield as he reviewed the statement before him. *Pretty much the same as she told me yesterday*, he thought. He took a deep drag on his cigarette and then went to the door and motioned for Betty to bring Sylvia in.

Sylvia was wearing a khaki skirt with a bright red top and a pair of strappy high-heel sandals. She entered the room with the receptionist, who said, "Mrs. Winston, Detective St. John."

Gabe responded, "Thank you, Betty. Please see that I am not disturbed."

"Will do, Detective," Betty said as she left the room, closing the door behind her.

"Have a seat, Sylvia. This shouldn't take too long. I know you have to get back with the children."

"I'm in no hurry, Gabe. The kids are with a neighbor, and she told me to take as long as I needed."

"How are they doing? How did they take the news of Zane's death?"

"Hard, Gabe, hard. They were crying all morning and were still crying when I left them with the Fletchers."

Gabe, feeling genuinely sorry for the children, said, "Sylvia, please sit down so I can get you out of here soon." Personally, he wanted to get rid of Sylvia as quickly as possible, yet he had to do his job and obtain a thorough statement from her.

Sylvia situated herself in the chair at the small table between them, and Gabe began questioning her. A half hour into the interview, Gabe said, "Sylvia, you show no remorse, no sadness, no tears about Zane's death. People will pick up on that, you know, and wonder if you may have had something to do with your husband's murder."

She looked directly at him and said, "It's as I told you last night. I loved Zane well enough, but I didn't like him. I mean, he fathered my children, and for that I loved him. But he was a snake. He was after anything in a skirt while I sat home with the kids. We hadn't had sex for months. In fact, we didn't even sleep in the same bed. He'd been sleeping in the spare bedroom for the past five or six months. I reacted to him by drinking and spending money, both of which I'm going to try to curtail for the children's sake."

Gabe looked across the small table and said, "I think we're finished. You had better get home. The children need your support."

Sylvia lit a Philip Morris and settled back into her chair. Gabe felt his crotch being rubbed. He looked under the table and saw Sylvia's brightly red painted toes massaging the rising bulge in his pants. "Sylvia! We can't do this. We can't. We can't ever again. It's not allowed, and I could lose my job."

She continued, saying, "Unzip your pants." Feeling the strain between his legs mounting, he reached down and unzipped his fly. Gabe did not wear underwear, so as soon as he was unzipped, his erection was free. Sylvia wasted no time. She had her other sandal off and began masturbating Gabe with her feet. In a matter of moments, Gabe reached an intense orgasm, ejaculating on her bare feet. "Oh God! This has to stop."

Sylvia smiled. "Do you have a napkin or a rag."

"What?" Gabe replied as he regained his senses. "Oh no, no, nothing."

"Okay," Sylvia said. "I'll just have to wear you home."

"Sylvia, we have to stop this."

"It's like old times. Stop by tonight," she said as she exited the room.

Gabe readjusted himself, lit a cigarette, and thought, *Jesus, that was something.* What made it all the more intense was the excitement of possibly being caught. The lieutenant or anyone else could have walked in on them—and then what? The repercussions would have been severe.

The detective regained his composure and began going over Sylvia's signed statement. Nothing really there, as he suspected. She married Zane for a name and for money. She loved him for fathering her children, Brad and Caroline. But that could not overcome the hurt and disappointment and even the hate she felt for Zane for his continuous unfaithfulness. There was nothing to implicate Sylvia in the murders. She stated that her neighbor, Eloise Fletcher, saw her at about four o'clock as she was sitting and drinking on her back patio. Sylvia had waved and spoken to Eloise. Gabe would verify that with Ms. Fletcher tomorrow, and that would be it for eliminating Sylvia as a suspect. But what about eliminating Sylvia as an old flame reunited? He would have to work on that problem.

Gabe left the interview room around one o'clock and was walking across the large detective room when the receptionist intercepted him. "Gabe, the lieutenant left, but he called the FBI, and an agent will be here for a meeting at nine o'clock in the morning to go over the case."

"Okay, thanks, Betty. I'll be here." With that, he proceeded out of the station, got into his car, and drove off.

7

Thomas Atherton finished his shower and was dressed by eight thirty. He had spent the time after his shower pouring over the packet of material on Victor Marchenko and trying to reach Carl Waters, to no avail. "Christ," he said, "that whore can't be that good." He then was reminded of the tenderness between his own legs as he showered. "Well, okay, maybe." Atherton had been reading and rereading the Marchenko file for three and a half hours. He knew that Marchenko had been selected to be educated at Moscow University and that he was from the Ukraine, where his father had been a midlevel party functionary until his untimely death from a heart attack in 1942. Victor, at that time, had completed his studies and had been awarded the doctorate in physics, but he had returned home to settle his father's estate rather than accepting a coveted position in the one of the Soviet military directorates. Apparently, Victor knew that a job would be waiting for him in Moscow. However, the Germans had other ideas, and in the summer of 1942, Hitler set the Wehrmacht on the Soviet Union in Operation Barbarossa. Marchenko was swept up in this onslaught when his village was inundated with armed men wearing gray-green uniforms. Victor plead that he was a physicist who could be useful to the German's war machine. The British sergeant, whose men were indiscriminately killing the civilians in the village, ordered Marchenko spared. He was transported to Berlin, where he remained for eight months before being transported to Peenemünde, a secret base situated on a German island in the Baltic Sea, to work on the V-2 missile program. There, he provided valuable research and development on optics and guidance systems for the V-2 rocket. He remained at Peenemünde until the Allies arrived in 1944 and liberated the facility. Once again, Victor Marchenko was swept up in the liberation. He, Von Braun, and scores of other German physicists and engineers were sent to the United States, where they spent time in Washington, DC, and Virginia being debriefed. They were then sent to Lawrence Livermore, Los Alamos, and other government laboratories to work at developing the missile for America.

Marchenko was singled out for work in Ohio at Winston Optics in Putnam Landing. Winston Optics had a lucrative contract to work on parts of the Norton bomb site. But as the war wound down in Europe, the War Department looked ahead to missile development, which required not only optics but guidance systems based upon gyroscopes, and Victor Marchenko's expertise, as he had been largely responsible for guiding the V-2s to London, as well as for the devastation and resulting loss of life.

Marchenko's American handlers transported him to Winston's Optical Factory in Putnam Landing in late 1946. Zane Winston was told what the new contract would entail, and Uncle Sam expanded the optics laboratory at Winston Optics, paid Marchenko's salary, expanded security with additional Ohio National Guardsman, and purchased a house for him just farther north on Overlook Drive. The house had been purchased at a premium from a family of a wealthy, eccentric resident. It was high on a hill overlooking the Elk Eye River. Marchenko was provided an armed driver to transport him back and forth and to stay in the house for protection. What Marchenko discovered, but told no one, was that the eccentric millionaire who built the house in the 1920s had a secret tunnel constructed down to the Elk Eye River. The federal agents discovered this fact when they researched the property prior to purchasing the house for Marchenko in 1946.

They found that Harry Fox, a prominent contractor in Putnam Landing, had built the house for Mr. Atha. They tracked Fox down in Putnam Landing, now retired and an old man, and interviewed him for over an hour. When the interview had ended and the agents were leaving his home, he stopped them. "You know, boys," he said as he filled his pipe from his tobacco pouch and lit it, the strong, sweet smell of tobacco smoke reaching the agents' nostrils. They halted and swung around to face Mr. Fox again. "I've never told anybody this. In fact, I was sworn to secrecy these many years ago when I worked for Mr. Atha. Well, you boys, being federal agents and all of that, and what with this awful war going on, I reckon that I can tell you. Besides, everyone else is dead or might as well be."

The two agents looked at each other quizzically and then at Mr. Fox. Then one of them said, "What's this you are saying?"

"Huh, yes, sir," he went on as he puffed on his pipe, "old Mr. Atha paid me a lot of money to dig him a secret tunnel from the basement of the house down to the Elk Eye. Yes, sir, a lot of money and a lot more to keep my mouth shut about it. I selected five of my best men, including a mining engineer who had worked in the West Virginia coal fields and who knew about deep mines and how to excavate them. He did a wonderful job. That tunnel goes seven hundred feet and almost twenty feet below the street coming out of the bank just under the Pennsylvania railroad tracks. There's a front door of solid steel forged at the old Blandy Foundry at the exit. We planted trumpet vines to grow up and hide the door. To my knowledge, no one has ever discovered this. And why the old man wanted it built I'll never know."

"Are you saying there's a tunnel down to the river?" one of the agents asked.

"Yes, sir," the old man replied, puffing on his pipe, "and with electric lights all the way down to the door."

"What the hell! Well, what was it for?" the agent asked.

The old contractor replied, "Sir, I do not know. Mr. Atha paid me so much money that I never asked. We worked on that for months. At some point, I didn't think we were going to be able to finish it. I paid my crew very well for secrecy. I do not believe that any one of them ever divulged anything about that tunnel. Sadly, all five of these men are dead. I don't think there's anyone left except me who knows about it. Old Mr. Atha died in the thirties, and his two daughters may not have known about it. Anyway, one of them died, and the other went crazy and is in the insane asylum in Columbus, so there's no one left except me, and I figured that you two, being federal agents, should know."

"Yes, thank you, sir, for your honesty," they replied as they left the house.

This entire interview was included verbatim in the file that Atherton had spent over three hours going over. He stopped reading, lit a cigarette, and called Waters again.

Just as Thomas hung up the telephone, the doorbell rang. Atherton looked through the peephole to discover Carl standing on the other side of the door. He opened the door, saying, "Where the hell have you been? I've been trying to reach you all morning."

"I've been doing the same thing as you, you dumb bastard," Carl retorted. "Did you receive a package?"

"Yes," Atherton said. "Come sit down at the table." Atherton motioned with his hand. "We have much to do."

Atherton and Waters devoted the remainder of the day to reading, rereading, discussing, and planning how to complete this assignment. Around eight o'clock, Atherton's phone rang. It was the colonel, calling to see if the package had arrived and if the two were working on it. Atherton told him that they had been working on it all day and that things were coming together. "Excellent," the colonel replied. "You are scheduled to depart Dulles at 10:00 a.m. on TWA Flight 1317 for Columbus, Ohio. Your tickets will be at the TWA counter. Also, in Columbus, there will be a car waiting for you at the airport. It will be parked on the second level of the parking garage in space number 23. The keys will be on the sun visor. Do you understand?"

"Yes, sir, Colonel," Atherton said. "We will be ready."

"Very well, gentlemen. Have a good trip," he replied sardonically.

That bastard, Thomas thought as he hung up the telephone. "We leave at 10:00 a.m. on Tuesday, and this time they're providing a car."

8

The alarm clock rang at seven o'clock Monday morning in Detective St. John's bedroom. He sat up and turned it off before going into the bathroom for a shower and getting dressed. "God, I feel rested after a good night's sleep," he said as he left the apartment for Kate's Diner.

Kate was her usual motherly self as she fussed over Gabe and served him breakfast. "What you need is a good woman to take care of you, Gabe. I would do it myself if I was twenty-five years younger, but I'm not, and you need to find yourself a nice girl and settle down. One who would take care of you and fix your breakfast and have dinner ready and be there for you."

"Now don't start that, Kate. You know that if I can't have you, I don't want anybody." She was always trying to play the matchmaker for Gabe, suggesting eligible women in Putnam Landing who she believed would make Gabe an excellent wife.

"Well, I told you if I were twenty-five years younger and old Pete wasn't in the picture, you wouldn't stand a chance."

Gabe laughed, finished his breakfast and left for the police station. It was 8:20 a.m. when he entered the station house. After saying good morning to Betty, the receptionist, he opened the door into the detective room and made his way to Lieutenant George's office. To his surprise, as he entered the office, the FBI agent was already there.

"Gabe, good morning. Chester Matthews of the FBI is the agent in charge. Chet, you know Gabriel St. John, the detective in charge of this case?" Lieutenant George said.

"Yes. Hi, Chet," Gabe said, shaking the agent's hand. "I wasn't sure it would be you here this morning. I thought there would be someone here from Columbus or maybe even Washington, DC."

"Nope, it's just me. At this stage, we want to see what you have and what may be involved."

Gabe had worked with Chester Matthews several years before on a local embezzlement case, and he didn't like him too much. He thought that Chester was too much of a God-fearing, flag-waving, McCarthyite Republican, and this got in the way of solving crimes. Lieutenant George knew this. He tried to smooth things over and mediate between the two lawmen. "Well now, you two boys know each other and will have to get to the bottom of these murders. I must admit this is a real stumper for Putnam Landing. We've got two bodies, a radio, some guns, and at this point, that's it."

"Well, Lieutenant," Agent Matthews responded, "that's what this great nation, our president, and the Bureau are for. We have resources available to us that small law enforcement departments can only dream of, and God willing, we'll solve this case."

Gabe sat at the corner of the desk rolling his eyes, listening to what he considered the bullshit spewing out of Agent Matthews mouth.

Lieutenant George said, "Well, gentlemen, very well. Those are the kinds of resources we need to solve this thing, so can we get started?"

In the Virginia apartment of Thomas Atherton, the two operatives were planning for how they were going to kill Dr. Marchenko. "We have to hit him and get out," Carl said. "It has to be fast with no fuckups like with the woman and her boyfriend."

"I agree," Thomas replied. "But we must observe him and learn his habits. We'll have to watch his goings and comings back and forth from home to work. I think we might want to take a rifle with us."

"What about the Russians, the KGB? Will we have any competition when we get there?" Carl asked.

"I don't know. We know they want him back or dead. We know they're after the technical specifications and the plan for that guidance system. That's why that Hungarian delegation was visiting the factory. Binoculars and telescopes, my ass. They're after those plans, and if they get Marchenko, they've got his brain and the guidance system. If they don't get him, they kill him, depriving us of the completed system. At least for a period of time. That's why we've got to get him first. We know that he and that bitch were somehow working together, but we don't know how much she was able to pass on."

"Well," Carl said, "we don't have to worry about her any longer."

It was ten thirty at night when Carl and Atherton finished their Sunday meeting. "Tomorrow, we'll visit the colonel for any last-minute instructions and to apprise him of what we'll be doing in Ohio and get any equipment and information we need. Then on Tuesday morning, we'll head out."

"Okay, Tom, I'll see you in the morning."

They arrived at the colonel's brownstone at eight thirty Monday morning. Hans showed them into the colonel's study, where he greeted them over a cup of coffee and a Camel. "Good morning, gentlemen. It's a beautiful morning out there."

"Yes, it is, Colonel Corbin," Atherton quickly responded. All Thomas and Carl wanted was to get their business over and get out.

"Coffee, gentlemen?" the colonel asked.

Both responded, "Yes." Hans poured two cups.

"This is wonderful java," the colonel said. "It's a full-body Colombian. Wonderful stuff." Atherton thanked Hans as he passed the cup to him. He lit a Chesterfield as the colonel asked, "Have you two read the dossier on Dr. Marchenko?"

"We have," Atherton responded before taking a sip of the hot, dark coffee. "Ah, Colonel, you are right; this is good stuff."

Colonel Corbin smiled and gave a slight nod as he extinguished his cigarette in what appeared to be an antique vase saucer, which he was using as an ashtray. "Let's hear what you've come up with."

For the next hour and a half, Atherton and Waters explained their plan to Colonel Corbin, how they were going to watch and observe, selecting the best place for a kill shot. At the end of this discussion, Atherton said, "You know, Colonel, I've been wondering just how you're so sure that Marchenko was working with this Diane Smith. I mean, where's the hard evidence? There was nothing in that dossier indicating that they were working together. There was nothing showing that they had even been in the same town or the same place together. Nothing. Nothing solid. Nothing showing that they knew each other."

Colonel Corbin sat back in his chair and lit a cigarette. His eyes narrowed as he glared at Atherton. After a long pause, he responded with an edginess in his voice bordering on anger, "goddamn it! You two are mechanics, and you don't need to know what caused the hole in the oil pan. You just have to fix it. That's what you're being paid to do. Fix it! You have all the information you need. The rest is on a need-to-know basis, and you don't need to know."

"Yes, Colonel," Atherton quickly replied. "We have no problem doing the job, and it will be done."

"Good, Thomas. I suspect no more mistakes," he said as he leaned forward in his chair, placing his elbows on the large Chippendale desk.

"Don't worry, Colonel. Carl and I will do the job and will be back within the week." The two men rose from their chairs to leave.

"Good," the colonel replied. "Oh, by the way, we have heard that Moscow is sending a team to kidnap or kill him as well. That's what the chatter says. So you two may have company on this job. Be careful and take care of business," he said as Atherton and Waters left the study.

As they closed the study door behind them, they looked at each other. Carl rolled his eyes, and Thomas shook his head. Outside, as the two got into Atherton's Jaguar, Thomas commented, "You know, Carl, there's just something about this whole thing that doesn't sit right with me."

Waters looked at Atherton and shrugged his shoulders as if to say, "Damned if I know."

Lieutenant George, Agent Matthews, and Detective St. John spent the morning going over the case. "The radio is definitely Russian," Agent Matthews stated. "The CZ is also of Iron Curtain origin. These are issued to the East German Stasi, though we have been informed that the Russians have developed a new sidearm based upon this pistol." The agent picked up the Walther. "It's supposedly chambered in a 9 mm round; however, they are not yet available to their satellite countries. Right now, though, I am interested in the woman."

Detective St. John took the lead, explaining that her name was Diane Smith and that she had been in Putnam Landing approximately five years. This entire time, she had worked at Winston Optics, where she rose through the ranks very rapidly to become Zane Winston's right-hand man. "We know they were sleeping together and that she may have become the power behind the throne at the company. We also know that she graduated from Ohio State in 1950 and that Zane hired her in 1951."

Agent Matthews raised his right hand and interjected, "What was her major at OSU?"

Gabe thought for a moment, trying to remember. Then he recalled finding her diploma in one of the drawers. "Oh, yes, I do recall now. It was engineering or physics, one of those. I remember thinking that most women went into art or cooking or something like that, not science or engineering or such. Those are for male students."

"Yes, well, Detective, do you have any other background on her? For example, where she's from? Where was her home? What about her travels? Friends? Acquaintances? Anything else?"

Lieutenant George said, "Agent Matthews, the murders happened on Friday afternoon as nearly as we can tell. The bodies weren't discovered until Saturday morning. Yesterday being Sunday, we were not in the office except for two interviews, that of the girl who found the bodies and Mr. Winston's widow. This being Monday morning, we're now on the case."

"Well, Lieutenant, that may be the way a small-town department works, but the Bureau never sleeps," Agent Matthews retorted. "We work twenty-four hours a day, seven days a week, to solve a case."

"What! What the fuck are you saying?" Gabe St. John yelled as he rose from his chair.

As he was stammering to find more words, Agent Matthews calmly said, "Please, Detective. Our director, Mr. Hoover, does not condone the use of profanity of any sort, and quite frankly, I find it to be offensive and against my strong Methodist upbringing, so please refrain from that vulgar language."

Gabe was seething. He wanted to leap across to where Matthews was sitting and strangle that pompous, Bible-thumping son of a bitch. Just as he was about to open his mouth, Lieutenant George intervened. "Gabe," he said firmly, "do we have anything back from the coroner yet?"

"No, not yet. Yesterday was Sunday, you know. No autopsies on Sunday."

"Well," said Agent Matthews, "I'll run the background on the woman and the radio and make some other inquiries regarding the case. Can we meet again on Thursday morning? Maybe the autopsies will have been completed by then. In the meantime, you fellows know where to reach me should you need anything. Until then, good day to you both." With that, the agent left Lieutenant George's office.

"I swear to you, Roy," St. John said as he paced the office, shaking his head, "if I had known they would send that pompous son of a bitch to us, I never would have suggested that you call them," Gabe said as he lit a cigarette.

"I know," Roy George replied, "but this case has all the markings of an international incident. Maybe it even has national security concerns, so at some point the FBI will have to be involved."

"Yeah, I know. You're right about that, but that Matthews is such a straitlaced prick," Gabe said, then took a drag of the Chesterfield.

"Gabe, you've got to work with him, and so do I, so enough about him and get on with your job."

"Okay. I'm off to lunch and then to Winston Optics and also to that Fletcher woman, that neighbor of Silva's."

"You know Sylvia from high school, don't you?"

"Yes. We were in the same class."

Lieutenant George said, "Don't let that get in your way—if you know what I mean."

"No, no, no, Lieutenant, you're right. Don't worry, I won't." With that, Gabe left the office and headed to lunch.

Following lunch, the afternoon went routinely. Gabe went to Winston Optics around one thirty in the afternoon to interview the employees, especially Dr. Marchenko. To his dismay, Marchenko did not report for work that Monday morning. The woman in charge of the personnel office, Ms. Nina Black, was quite helpful, as she gave the detective Marchenko's home address and telephone number. "You know, Detective, we really don't know much about Dr. Marchenko," she said. "He's one of those *special* employees. We have nothing in the personnel file except for his address and phone number. He just appeared here. He was brought by two men wearing suits and looking very professional. They brought him to my office and said that he would be working here. When I asked about his background information, one of the men said, 'There is nothing more that you need.' They were very abrupt, but I didn't think too much of it, as during the war, we had several men working here with no personnel files. You know, I think it was just part of the war effort and our contracts with the government."

Gabe said, "Well, what's he like and where he is he from?"

"Truthfully, Detective, the man is an enigma. Nobody knows anything about him. He keeps to himself. He has no close friends in the plant. He arrives around seven thirty and leaves around six. He is friendly. And by that, I mean if you pass him in the hall or see him in the lunchroom, he will speak. He'll say hello or good morning, but that's it. He eats alone. He goes back and forth to work alone, and he has a heavy accent. Other than that, I know nothing about him."

"Well, Ms. Black, I am going to need to talk with him."

"Detective St. John, this is a very bad time to talk with anyone here. We're all devastated about Mr. Winston and Ms. Smith. We're just going through the motions today. I'm sure you understand."

"Oh, yes, of course, Ms. Black, but I have a double homicide to deal with, and I must talk with people here at the plant. What can you tell me about Diane Smith?" the detective asked as he lit a cigarette.

"Oh, yes, her, uh," the personnel officer mumbled as she opened her large desk drawer and sifted through her files until she arrived at Diane Smith's. As she extracted the file from the drawer, she said, "Well, again, Detective, not too much."

"Now, what do you mean by not too much, Mrs. Black?" Gabe said, somewhat agitated.

"Well, Detective, I'll show you what I have. It's not much. We know that she was a graduate of Ohio State in 1950. Mr. Winston hired her in 1951 to work in the lab, and she has been here since then. I really don't know where she came from other than that. Rumor has it that she lived in Europe before coming to the US, but I don't know that for sure. She was kind of a cold fish unless she wanted something. Then she was your best friend, if you know what I mean."

The detective, looking somewhat puzzled, said, "I'm not sure that I'm following you."

"Detective St. John, I'm not sure that I can explain it to you, but after she was hired, she would interact with other employees. If you would meet her in the hall and speak to her, she would only nod and smile—no hello, just a nod. Well, one day after she had been here for about a year, or a year and a half perhaps, she appeared in my office just after lunch. She was all smiles and warmth. She treated me like a long-lost sister and said that she wanted to transfer out of the Commercial Optical Laboratory and into Dr. Marchenko's laboratory. I told her that on the face of it, that was impossible. I explained that Dr. Marchenko pretty much worked alone and that if she wanted to work with him, she would have to talk to him and Mr. Winston. She became slightly agitated, telling me that, as a personnel officer, I could make the transfer. I explained that I could not do that and she would have to talk to Dr. Marchenko and Mr. Winston to make that happen. She then made what I thought a strange request. She asked to see Dr. Marchenko's personnel file. I could not believe it. I flat out said no. She became extremely upset. She was yelling at me, saying that if I knew what was good for me, I would grant her request. At that point, I opened the door to my office and showed her out. She never gave me the time of day after that.

"Then in April 1952, there was a conference in Pittsburgh, and Mr. Winston attended, and so did she. Shortly after they returned, Mr. Winston entered my office and informed me that Ms. Smith was now his assistant. He told me to make the changes and to reflect a sizable pay raise. I did it, and believe me, she exercised her newfound authority. People at the plant did not like her. And another thing—Diane was always trying to befriend Dr. Marchenko. She was always trying to talk to him and trying to get him to show her his laboratory. I'm telling you, he would have no part of that woman. Well, he wouldn't have anything to do with anyone else, except for Mr. Winston, but especially not her."

Detective St. John sat for a few seconds, processing what Nina Black had told him before rising from his chair and stubbing out his cigarette in the ashtray. "Ms. Black, you have been helpful, and I may be back to talk with you further, but at this point, I think we are finished."

As Gabe exited the personnel office and went down the stairs to the first floor, he began to roam around. Seeing a door leading to the loading dock and the rear of the plant, he went through it and entered into a large storeroom and loading dock area. Stepping out onto the dock, he saw men loading two trucks with wooden crates. There was a railroad spur in the back of the plant, and on the dock was a stack of crates awaiting the train's arrival. When he was about to leave, he heard a voice calling, "Detective! Hey, Detective!" As he looked in the direction of the voice, he saw a thin, wiry older man dressed in dungarees and a T-shirt, busy loading boxes and crates. He had a full beard with a curve-stemmed pipe in the corner of his mouth. He called out, "You're a detective with the Putnam Landing Police, are you not?"

"Yes," Gabe replied, "I'm Detective Gabriel St. John."

The older man looked Gabe up and down before speaking. "Well, I'm Clem Ford, and I have worked on this loading dock for twenty-eight years."

"Well, I'm sure you must know your job very well," Gabe responded, not sure what else to say.

The older man approached Gabe, puffing on his pipe. "Yep, you bet I do. But that ain't why I stopped you."

"Well, okay," Gabe responded. "How can I help you?"

"You know, young fellow, this is a horrible mess. Mr. Winston was a really good fellow. I mean, he looked out for and took care of his employees, and almost every man here loved that man. For example, when I was laid up with surgery ten years ago, I was off work for three months, but I never missed a paycheck. That's just how he treated his employees, and now he's dead. Murdered. It ain't right, and it smells of that woman, Ms. Smith."

"How do you mean, Mr. Ford?" Gabe said.

"Well, Detective," Clem Ford continued, "that woman was no good. She was evil, wanton, and poor Mr. Winston never knew what hit him. And that poor Mrs. Winston and those children. That Smith woman was evil, I tell you, and she seduced Mr. Winston and screwed her way right into that job."

St. John, playing the devil's advocate, said, "Now, Mr. Ford, half the men in this town who are in the position of power and wealth have something on the side, and there is no law against that."

Ford, feeling a little inferior in this discussion, and a bit embarrassed at what he had just said, shuffled his stance, replying, "You may be right about that, Detective. I don't know. I'm just a dock monkey here at the plant. I don't know these people or how they live, but I am telling you that that woman was up to something. She wasn't what she was cracked up to be."

Gabe stared at Clem Ford for several seconds, saying nothing. Then he said, "Mr. Ford, exactly what are you saying?"

"Ms. Smith was always poking her nose in where it didn't belong. That is, she was always trying to get information out of everyone. For example, with Dr. Marchenko, she was always trying to warm up to him. You know, be friendly with him, but he wanted none of her. Especially, after they had that blow up in the parking lot one afternoon. He was so upset that he began yelling in some other language, German or Russian maybe. Do you know what? She answered him in that same language and never gave it a second thought until she saw me heading for my car to go home. Then she became very quiet, turned from Dr. Marchenko, and hurriedly walked away."

"Wait a minute," Gabe said excitedly. "Are you telling me that Diane Smith spoke Russian?"

"No," Clem said. "Well, I really don't, well, I really don't know what language it was, but whatever it was that he was speaking, she was talking right with him."

"I see," Gabe replied, thinking, *This is starting to fall into place.* "Tell me, Mr. Ford, were you alone when you overheard this conversation?"

Clem jumped on that, saying, "It was no conversation like you and I are having. No, sir, they were a going at each other, and no, I was not alone. That young fella Ernie Cobb was walking out to his car with me."

"Where can I find Ernie Cobb?"

"I wouldn't know, as about month or so ago, he just quit coming to work. Word on the dock is that he got fired."

"Fired?" St. John asked. "Was he a good employee?"

"No, sir, he wasn't, and she got rid of him."

"How could Ms. Smith do that on her own?"

"Don't know, Detective, but she had her ways." Clem hesitated, then went on. "Detective St. John, I am going to tell you something that as God is my witness I saw with my own eyes and have never told another living person. That argument I told you about happened on a Friday. Well, on Monday morning, Ernie and I were working by ourselves on that dock," he said, motioning to the dock. "They had the five other fellows off in another part of the plant doing something, so that just left me and Ernie. Now there were two heavy crates that had to be moved from over there"—he motioned with his thumb—"to the far back of the storeroom out onto the dock. We had a truck coming in at ten thirty to pick them up for transport to New Jersey. I remember that. Well, sir, those crates were big and heavy, and the truck drivers won't help load, and they don't like to wait." Clem lit his pipe. "I knew I was gonna need help, and I looked around for Ernie, but he was nowhere to be found. I started looking for him among the crates and boxes here in the storeroom, but he wasn't to be found. Then I thought maybe he was in the restroom and set off to check in there. As I got to the restroom entrance—there's no door, you know, but we don't really need one the way the entrance is laid out—I heard these awful moans and mumbling. When I turned the corner, there stood Ernie with his back against the wall, his pants down on the floor. On her knees in front of him was Diane Smith. She had his member in her mouth and was bobbing her head back and forth like she was at a Halloween party going for apples. She had her back to me, and he had his eyes closed, so I just quietly backed out of the bathroom and went back to the crates. I'll tell you, I have never seen anything like that here, and I've been here twenty-eight years."

"God almighty," Gabe responded, feigning shock at what he had just been told while remembering his episode with Sylvia the day before. "What happened then? Did you say anything to Ernie?"

"No, sir. Not a word. We moved the crates, and he was there for about two weeks, and then he was gone. Rumor has it that he was fired, but I don't know that for sure." Mr. Ford knocked the ashes and cottle out of his pipe against one of the crates.

St. John, a little bewildered by all that he had just heard, said, "I don't suppose you know where this Ernie Cob lives, do you?"

"No, sir, I do not. Ernie was a friendly enough sort and not really a good employee, I guess, but he never divulged too much about himself, and I never asked. Maybe that's why we got along."

"Mr. Ford, you have been most helpful, and I may want to talk to you again."

"Well, you know where to find me, Detective. I'll help you all I can to find out who killed Mr. Winston."

"Thank you, Mr. Ford. I'll be in touch." Gabe turned and walked out of Winston Optics.

As he got into the car, Gabe lit a cigarette and picked up the radio to call the station. Betty, the receptionist, wore two hats at the Putnam Landing Police Station. She was the greeter receptionist and functioned as the dispatcher answering radio calls between and among officers and the station. Betty responded to Gabe's call for information on Ernie, probably Ernest, Cobb. He then started the engine of his V8 Ford, listening to it rumble before placing it in gear and heading for the Fletcher residence.

It was nearly three o'clock when Gabe pulled into the Fletchers' driveway. He observed the Winston house as he drove past it, but there was no sign of Sylvia and the kids. As he approached the front stoop of the Fletcher house, it too appeared lifeless, but just as he was about to ring the doorbell, the door flew open, and there stood a woman who appeared to be in her thirties. She was barefooted, wearing a pair of shorts and sleeveless top. A cigarette dangled from between her bright red lips, and she held a highball in her left hand. Her hair and makeup appeared to be perfect. Her long fingers were painted red at the nails, as were her toenails. Before Gabe could get any words out, Mrs. Fletcher stated, "I am Eloise Fletcher, Detective. Sylvia told me that you might be calling on me. Come in. Come in. Can I get you a drink?"

"Well, thank you, and no thank you to the alcohol. I'm on duty, you know," Gabe stammered, somewhat taken off guard by this gregarious woman.

"Yes, of course. Well, please come in and sit down. Make yourself comfortable. If you don't mind, I'll just refresh mine," she said as she stubbed out the cigarette in a coffee table ashtray.

"No, no, please, go right ahead. I'll just wait here. Take your time and be comfortable, Mrs. Fletcher." Gabe watched Eloise Fletcher glide across the living room and disappear into the kitchen. She was a rather large woman, tall with good legs and a great body. *Nicely put together*, he thought as she was returning to the living room with a full glass. "Now, how can I help you, Detective?" She sat down in a chair and put her feet up.

"Well, Mrs. Fletcher—"

"Whoa," she interrupted. "No, Detective. Stop with that Mrs. Fletcher bullshit. Call me Eloise."

"Okay ... Eloise, how did you know who I was? I mean, we've never met, have we?"

"No, damn it, but I've seen you over at Sylvia's, and she told me who you were."

"Well, that answers that," Gabe said.

Eloise continued, "This whole situation is just one hell of a mess and a tragedy, and to think that it happened right here in little ole Putnam Landing."

"I couldn't agree with you more, Eloise, and that's why I'm here, to help clear up some things and establish an alibi."

"What do you mean?" she said, taking a long pull of her drink and lighting another Lucky.

Gabe lit a cigarette and replied, "Well, Eloise, you know how cops are; we like to tie up loose ends."

"And Sylvia is a loose end. Am I right?"

"Well, yes, she is," Gabe said. They both took drags of their cigarettes, and Eloise took a long drink of her highball.

"So, what do you want to know, Detective?"

"How well did you know Zane Winston?"

Eloise finished her cigarette and her highball. She leaned across the table to put out the cigarette, and as she did, Gabe could see down the front of her top, revealing two lovely, bare breasts. She straightened up before replying, "Detective St. John, allow me to refresh my drink prior to answering that."

"Help yourself."

When she returned with her glass refilled, she sat down in her chair. Folding one leg under her, she lit another Lucky and began. "You're Gabe, right?" Gabe nodded. "What I am about to tell you, I have never told another soul, and for my sake, I hope you'll never tell anyone."

"Eloise, I cannot tell anyone what happens between us." *What a slip,* he thought. *What are you thinking?* "I mean, well, what I mean is this interview is private."

"Yeah, yeah, okay, then let's move on. One night, about a year and a half ago, I couldn't sleep, so around three o'clock in the morning, I got up and came downstairs to have a hit of vodka, thinking that might help. Well, I'm sitting at the kitchen table drinking the vodka when I see headlights pull into the Winstons' drive. I didn't think too much of that. I just thought that Zane was coming home after drinking. A few seconds later, there was knocking on the side door of the back screened-in porch." She motioned toward the back of the house where a large screened-in porch extended the entire length of the house.

"I was in the kitchen, so I went out to answer the door. It was Zane. He was fairly drunk, and I let him in. He said, smiling, 'My house is all dark, so I came to the light.' He had a big schoolboy grin. Then I realized that, from the light coming through the kitchen window, he could see right through this short, transparent baby doll negligee I was wearing. I turned to go back into the house, but he grabbed me and pulled me to him. He kissed me hard and deeply. I don't need to go into any graphic details, but suffice it to say, we made love—well, really, we fucked in every conceivable way until five o'clock that morning."

Eloise had become quite animated. She was pacing around the coffee table, gesturing with her arms and smoking. "Honestly, I hadn't felt that satisfied in years. After he left, I realized that he had not worn any protection, so, let me tell you, I had a few anxious moments that month, but it all turned out okay." She took a long drink of her vodka and lit another cigarette before continuing. "The affair lasted until six months ago when he just stopped coming around. I guess I was just too much woman for him," she said with a smile. Detective St. John responded with a smile and a slight nod.

Eloise went to the kitchen to pour another drink. When she walked back into the living room, Gabe noticed a misstep in her gait. The alcohol was affecting her. She now sat down next to Gabe on the sofa as she lit another cigarette and took a long pull of her vodka. "You know, Detective, it's not like he was the greatest lover of all times. It was the sheer excitement of the whole thing. The risk, the fear of being caught in the act of having sex with Zane when people were around. Like that first time. Christ, Harry and the kids were sound asleep right above us. Another time was our annual Christmas party. I was in my ivory wool sweater and a short wool red-and-green skirt, worn with green high heels, hosting five couples for Yule festivities. We ran out of wine as we were singing Christmas carols and eating hors d'oeuvres. And, of course, the alcohol was flowing freely. The wine was getting low, so Harry, my husband, quietly commented to me that I needed to go to the basement to get more bottles. I went to the basement to get more, and as I kicked off my heels to get on the stool to reach the top-shelf bottles, I felt a hand up under my skirt. I yelled, but they didn't hear, as they were busy drinking, singing, and laughing. It was Zane. He removed my panties, hoisted my skirt up to my waist, helped me off the stool, and as I held on to the shelves, he entered me from behind, and God did I ever have an orgasm. All the people upstairs, including Harry, and there we were in the basement, screwing like two rabbits. I went back upstairs, sans panties and shoes, and the revelry never missed a beat. Later on that night, he tried to cull me out from the herd again, but Sylvia was watching him too closely, and we couldn't."

Gabe asked, "What do you mean by *cull me out from the herd?*"

"Oh, that. Well, you know, the way an alpha male in nature will cull out of the herd a female for breeding."

Gabe realized she was drunk. He had to be careful as he proceeded. "Eloise, how did it make you feel when Zane cut you off?"

"What do you mean?"

"Did you feel angry at being used by him and then discarded—those good times, those exciting times that you enjoyed, the attention that he paid you abruptly coming to an end? What was your reaction to that?"

"My reaction. Well, Gabe, my reaction, my reaction …"

"Well," Gabe went on, "anger, hurt, humiliation, what?"

Eloise lit a cigarette. "What in the hell are you leading up to? Are you asking me if I played the jilted lover and murdered Zane and his bimbo? My answer to that is hell no. Look, Detective, Zane was fun for me, like I was fun for him. I never expected more out of that fling than what I got. I knew Zane Winston, and I know his type. I knew that I was no more than a notch on his cock, but that's all he was to me. I'll move on, look for something else on the side, but I'm not brooding about an affair that has ended." She let her hand fall gently across the back of Detective St. John as she reached for her pack of Luckies on the coffee table.

"Eloise, can you tell me if you saw Sylvia on Friday afternoon in her backyard?"

Taken aback, Eloise took a drag of the Lucky while she tried to regroup. "Friday? What do you mean, Friday?"

"Sylvia, in her statement, maintained that on Friday, late afternoon, she spoke with you in the backyard. Do you recall this?"

She quickly shook her head, saying, "Friday? Friday?" Then she exclaimed, "Yes! Yes, she was out in her yard at least three different times—one trip to the garbage, one with her kids, and once when we spoke. It was late in the afternoon, and we talked about fixing dinner. It must have been about four."

With that, Gabe stood up, saying, "Well, Eloise, thank you so much for your time this afternoon. If there's anything else we need, I may be back."

Eloise stood up unsteadily, reaching down to the coffee table to gain her balance. Gabe was walking toward the door when she caught up to him, grabbing his arm to steady herself. She wrapped her arms around him and kissed him on the mouth. Her body was pressed hard against his, and he began to feel a response. He stopped her and pried her away from him. She quickly said, "Harry won't be home until seven, and the kids are at their grandparents' for the whole week."

"Eloise, I can't do this. Not now anyway. I have to go."

She responded with a hurt look, saying, "When?"

"I have to leave, but thank you for your time."

"Will you come back?" she longingly asked him.

"Maybe, sometime," he replied as he opened the door and left. *Jesus,* he thought, *what is it about these housewives?*

The two assassins landed at Port Columbus at one o'clock in the afternoon. They located the car in the parking, and after stowing their gear in the trunk, they headed east on Route 40. Atherton and Waters didn't converse much on the drive, and it was around three o'clock when they pulled into the parking lot of a motel just west of Putnam Landing. The building was well maintained, with the office and a restaurant in the center and two wings with runs of rooms extending out from this center. As Atherton parked the Buick and turned off the engine, he said, "I'll get the room. You wait here."

Carl said, "Why can't I get the room? Why can't I drive the car? Why is it always you? I feel like the hired help."

Atherton opened the car door while responding, "You heard the colonel; we're merely mechanics, and I'm the head mechanic."

"Head mechanic. Why are you the head mechanic? Because you're a college boy?" Carl asked with a raised voice.

As he stepped out and was closing the door, Atherton's retort was, "That's part of it."

Atherton knew that Carl was not capable of much other than killing. He came from very poor beginnings and then went into the army and killed Germans. He was very good at that. Carl had to be directed, and for the most part, he would do the job and do it well, yet there were those times, such as during the hit on the woman when he got his feet tangled up in the shoes in her closet. That could have been catastrophic, Thomas thought. He could have easily taken that round in the brain. Then what? That woman was a trained adversary who could have easily killed him, Atherton thought as he walked into the motel office. Thomas Atherton knew that in order for all to go as planned, he had to be in control of the situation.

They got situated in their room, number 10, the last room on the east wing of the motel. "I'm going to take a shower, Carl, and feel more human. How about you?"

"No, not for me now, Tom. I'm just going to relax."

Atherton was not sure that Carl ever showered, as at times the man became quite ripe. "Well, okay then. I'll see you in a few."

When Atherton got out of the shower with the towel wrapped around him, Carl was drinking whiskey. "Hey, Carl?" Thomas said. "We have to be our best for the morning and the rest of the week, so take it easy on that stuff."

"Don't worry, Tommy boy, don't worry. Old Carl is just having a bit of the hair of the dog to steady his nerves for what lies ahead. You know, Tommy." Atherton detested being called Tommy. "I've been thinking," Carl continued, "about what you said this morning when we left that motherfucker's house. Something doesn't smell right about this whole thing. I mean, why is he so interested in killing this scientist? Have you heard anything about this guy? I mean scuttlebutt from the top or anything?"

"No, Carl, no, I have not," Atherton replied. "I don't quite understand it myself. But we are mechanics, you know," he said with a slight smile.

Yuri Gregorov was a tall well-built, thirty-year-old product of the Soviet state. He originated from Stalingrad, and he was there when the Wehrmacht lay siege to the city in 1943. He survived that ordeal but emerged from it scarred and hardened. His entire family was killed by the Germans through starvation and disease. Yuri was alone and full of hate for Germans at the age of seventeen. To survive the siege, he had to become a scavenger. He had to leave the shelter of the basement of his family home and go out into the streets to search for food. His father had not allowed any of the family to leave the basement, lest they fall prey to German snipers. He had watched his two brothers and sister die from starvation and cholera. His mother, shot through the head when she stepped out into the sunshine of a beautiful spring morning. Only he and his father were left. Then one day in the late summer, his father left to try to locate food and potable water. He never returned. Yuri was alone. He remained in the basement for several days, but he knew if he was going to live and seek retribution for his family, he would have to leave the basement and find food and water. Revenge is a powerful motivator. So on the fourth night following his father's disappearance, he cautiously ventured out. Yuri reasoned that going out at night would be safer, as he would be less of a target for the German snipers hiding in the ruined buildings of Stalingrad.

On that very first night, he came upon what appeared to be a deserted German encampment about one mile from his basement sanctuary. There were three dead German soldiers sprawled out on the ground. From what he could tell, they had all been shot through the head. One of them carried a rifle with a telescopic sight, and Yuri picked this up, along with extra ammunition the soldier had been carrying. Cautiously, he moved around the area, gathering up whatever he could find. There was a half wheel of cheese, a loaf of bread, and three tins of sardines. He found a cloth bag and filled it with these items. He thought that might have been some sort of forward staging area where the soldiers could get a quick meal. He gathered up the canteens and ammunition from the dead men before carefully easing his way back to the basement.

Once in his sanctuary, he devoured a large slice of cheese, a can of sardines, and a large chunk of the bread. Realizing that this was going to have to last him, he stopped eating and took a long drink from one of the canteens. Yuri then began to examine the rifle. It appeared to be a standard German K96 8 mm issue rifle with a telescopic sight. *This must be a sniper's rifle. This is what has killed my family and so many other citizens and soldiers. I will turn this on them. I will take revenge in the name of Mother Russia.* And so he did. Yuri learned to use the rifle by killing

Germans, first at close range and then by playing with the telescope. He gradually extended the range out to approximately two hundred yards. He became an asset to the Soviet cause in Stalingrad. He killed twenty German soldiers before the Germans surrendered. He was selected for special training and was sent to Moscow to the NKVD facility where he was abused and used and formally trained to become one of the premier agents and assassins of the USSR. This was the man who was boarding a plane at the Moscow Airport bound for New York City and on to Putnam Landing, Ohio—his mission, to kill the traitor, Dr. Victor Marchenko, enemy of the state.

T he day seemed to fly by, and before Gabe St. John knew it, it was Thursday morning. He found himself in the lieutenant's office, along with Chief Cochran, drinking station house coffee and smoking a cigarette. They were waiting for Agent Matthews, which was strange, as Chester Matthews never kept anyone waiting. Gabe was relieved at the delay as he thought, *That makes the God-fearing prick a little more of a human being.*

They had waited nearly thirty minutes when Agent Matthews entered the office saying, "Good morning, gentlemen. I'm very sorry to be so late, but there were several last-minute and important details I was working on."

"Think nothing of it, Agent Matthews. I'm sure you were legitimately busy in helping us solve this case. We certainly do appreciate your help and that of the Bureau in this regard," Chief Cochran said. Leaning forward in his chair, he continued, "You boys do a fine job of protecting our great nation and keeping us all safe from our enemies."

Jesus Christ, Gabe thought, rolling his eyes and looking away. He was probably getting the last verse of scripture from Hoover. *For Christ's sake, old Cochran is running for mayor, and he just made his first stump speech.* The Republican Party had been bandying Cochran's name about as a possible candidate for mayor after he retired on January 2. But not for Gabe St. John. He would never vote for, as he referred to them, a stinking-ass Republican. Not after the good that Franklin Roosevelt had done for the country. Gabe would rather scratch shit with the chickens than vote for a Republican.

Agent Matthews quickly acknowledged Chief Cochran's praise and then proceeded with what he had learned about Diane Smith. "Well, gentlemen, she's most definitely not who she appeared to be. Her name was Deidra Schmidt, born in Baden-Baden in 1920. Her parents were Herman and Freda Schmidt. Her father fought for the Kaiser in the First World War and was severely wounded at Tannenbaum. The Russians captured him, nursed him back to health, and after many months, let him go. Following that experience, he became a die-hard Bolshevik advocating for Germany to follow Russia into communism. From what we understood, he was never much of a man after being wounded, if you get my drift. Yet in 1920, his wife gave birth to this Deidra."

The agent paused to take a drink of his coffee. "We know that her mother died in 1928 from consumption and that her father was killed in 1933 by the Nazis. They were living in Berlin at the time. We don't know what happened to Deidra following her father's death. She dropped off the face of the earth, only to reemerge in 1950 in BAUM, working as a secretary in their Department of Labor. She then relocated to Paris, where she attended the Sorbonne and then to Columbus, Ohio, to Ohio State for a graduate degree, summa cum laude, and to Putnam Landing to work in the Optics Factory. We know that the radio and pistol you discovered are of communist bloc origin. The radio is definitely Russian. It is a design that was commonly used by the military during the war. The CZ 50 is a pistol issued to the East German Stasi and is unavailable anywhere else. True, there is a new pistol coming on, but it is not available in the satellite countries as of yet."

"What the hell was she really doing here?" Lieutenant George questioned.

"That, Roy, is what we must find out," Chester Matthews sharply retorted.

Gabe interjected, "I suspect our answer lies in that Optics Factory with Dr. Marchenko."

"I think you're correct, Gabe. Now, I caution all of you: do not talk to the press. Those damn reporters will mess us up. Do not say anything pertaining to the hidden radio or anything else. Lieutenant George will handle the press and all reporters, refer them to him," Matthews finished up.

Atherton and Waters had spent their time carefully observing Victor Marchenko. They watched him come and go. They followed him discretely and cased his house while he was at work. They had to be careful, as Marchenko had a housekeeper who arrived at six o'clock in the morning and stayed until seven o'clock in the evening.

Try as they might, they could not locate the opening to the tunnel at the river. The two searched the bank by the railroad tracks by night so as not to arouse suspicion from the marina employees just across the tracks on the river. It was during one of these nighttime forays that Atherton noticed someone watching them. He was standing on a pier looking straight at them. It was almost as if he was daring them to see him and confront him. Atherton took this in stride and calmly said to Carl, in a low voice, "Nothing here. Time to move on."

Carl, who had been moving along the bank with a long stick, poking into the dirt to try to find the exit, said, "Why? We're just getting a good start."

"Carl, let's go," Atherton firmly repeated.

"Okay, okay, I'm coming," Carl whispered in a falsetto voice.

The two moved up to the berm of Linden Avenue where their car was parked. They got into the Buick, and Atherton started the engine and drove slowly north for about a quarter mile. He never took his eyes off that pier, but the figure had disappeared into the night. As Thomas turned around and pulled the car to the side of the road, Carl asked, "What the hell was that all about? I was just getting a good start."

"We were being watched, Carl."

"What? By whom?"

"I have no idea, but he was standing on the dock, silhouetted by the moonlight against the river as though he wanted us to see him.

Remember, the colonel warned us that we might have company on this mission, and I think he was right. We do."

"Holy shit," Carl said. "I didn't see anything."

"I know, but I did. That's why we left when we did. We must be extremely cautious and plan for a third party and possibly taking him out as well."

"Let's get back to the room and talk about this," Carl said.

"You're right. Let's go."

Detective St. John emerged from the meeting to be confronted by Betty. She had seven messages for him, all left by Sylvia Winston. He quickly perused them, saying, "Thanks, Betty. I'll get back to her as soon as I can."

"Gabe, she sounded desperate, as though she really needed to talk with you."

"I know, and I'll get to her."

"She's hurting. She needs to talk with you."

"Betty, I'll get to her as soon as I can, but right now I have some other priorities."

"Okay," Betty said. "I just thought you should know."

"Thanks a lot. I'll get to her." With that, he left the station and headed back to Winston Optics.

As Gabe drove, he reviewed the stack of callback notes that Betty had stuffed into his hands. *Need to see you. Where have you been? Why haven't you called me? I need to see you.* One caught his attention. It was from Denise Potts and read, *I remembered a tidbit, which may interest you. Please see me.*

He pulled into the parking lot of Winston Optics.

Ms. Black directed him to the laboratory of Dr. Marchenko, and Gabe spent the next two hours interviewing him, to no avail. He would not, or could not, divulge what he was developing, simply saying that the detective would need either national security clearance or approval from the government before he could talk to him. Gabe stressed the fact that he was dealing with a double homicide and that he needed answers. Finally, he resorted to saying, "Dr. Marchenko, your life may be in danger."

Victor Marchenko looked at the detective before replying, "What do you mean?"

"Well, sir, you're a Russian working for the United States government. Mother Russia doesn't care much for that. If they have located you, which they very likely have, they will kill you."

"Well, what about my protection?" Marchenko asked.

"Well, sir, we can only do so much with our limited staff."

Marchenko knew the Russians. He knew how they worked. If in fact they had located him, he was a marked man. Yet he still refused to divulge anything about his work. Gabe asked him if Zane Winston and Diane Smith knew about what he was doing.

Marchenko replied, "Mr. Winston knew exactly what I was developing. That woman knew nothing, at least from me, though she tried her best to find out. I never trusted her, and I told her nothing. Now, what Mr. Winston might have told her, I do not know—you know, pillow talk and all of that."

"Are you saying that he was sleeping with her?" Gabe asked coyly.

"Detective, are you just arriving at that conclusion? It was an open secret. Everybody in this town, not just this plant, knew that she was his mistress. Are you honestly telling me that you don't know that?"

Gabe, feeling somewhat uncomfortable at being faced with this known fact, stammered, "Well, I guess I have heard that."

"You *heard* that," Marchenko said through his thick accent. "Everyone in the county has heard that," Marchenko said in a condescending voice. "Why is it taking you so long to catch on?"

Detective St. John was momentarily thrown off by Marchenko's attitude. With a confused look and realizing that he was not about to get any information without the proper clearances, he halted the interview. However, he reiterated the warning that Marchenko might be in danger. "Thank you, sir. We will talk again later," he said, getting up from his chair to make his leave.

"Detective, just know that I cannot divulge to you or anyone else more than I have told you, not without the proper clearance."

"I do understand, but I have two murders that I must solve, Dr. Marchenko. I do appreciate your time."

"I was supposed to be there, you know?"

"What?" Gabe asked. "Where were you supposed to be?"

"At her apartment," Marchenko replied. "Thursday, late in the afternoon, Mr. Winston stopped by the lab. He told me to be at her apartment at Friday at four thirty for a meeting with the three of us. I told him I wasn't interested in that kind of meeting. He looked at me and said that it was not an option and that I was to be there. He was my boss, after all, so I told him I would be there."

Gabe asked, "What was the meeting about and why at Diane's apartment?"

"I have no idea. He didn't tell me. He just said be there, so I planned to be at her apartment; it was on my mind all day Friday. Finally, at about three thirty, Mr. Winston came in to the lab and said that I did not need to be with them and that we could talk about it later. I was so relieved. Do you realize, Detective, if I had been there, I would have been killed as well as those two?"

"My God, Doctor, you were supposed to be there. You were number three."

Victor Marchenko looked puzzled. He was used to finding and solving anomalies in physics and mathematics but not in everyday life.

Gabe exited the laboratory of Winston Optics.

When Gabe was pulling out of the parking lot onto Linden Avenue, he thought that he had better see Sylvia. He didn't want her raving to Betty about their times together. He headed for Northgate and Sylvia's house. He pulled into her driveway and walked to the front stoop. He noticed Eloise Fletcher in her front yard. She waved to him, saying, "Hi, Gabe! How are you doing?" He acknowledged her wave, observing that she was wearing a deep-green one-piece bathing suit that accentuated her voluptuous hourglass figure.

She is a handsome woman, he was thinking as the front door opened. Sylvia stood there with a scowl on her face.

"Hello, Sylvia," Gabe said.

"Well, well. If it isn't the local small-town dick who's trying to service every housewife in the city instead of trying to find out who killed my husband."

"Oh, Sylvia, nice to see you too."

"I saw your car over there the other day while her husband and kids were gone. Was she any good?"

It was plain to Gabe that Sylvia had been drinking too much. He noticed that she was dressed to go somewhere. She was wearing a teal skirt, a white blouse, and dark hose. "Are you getting ready to leave, Sylvia?" Gabe asked.

"I've already been. I had to meet with the lawyer this afternoon, and I'm just getting back."

Wow, Gabe thought, *she's lost track of time or has been taking gin and tonic intravenously*. "Where are the kids, Sylvia?"

"With Marg, my housecleaner. I didn't know what else to do with them, and Marg offered to watch them if I needed her, so I dropped them off at her house before going to meet with that slimy lawyer."

Gabe was feeling pangs of sorrow for the children as he said, "Don't they need to be with you? Their father is dead, and they need comfort and support from you."

"They're fine. Believe me, they're fine. Damn you. Where have you been? Why haven't you returned my calls? I needed to see you, to be with you. Where have you been?"

"Sylvia," Gabe said, "I have been working to solve a double homicide. I have been at it, even in my sleep, trying to put this whole thing together. I have a physicist who can't talk because of national security. I have a neighbor"—he motioned toward the Fletchers'—"who has provided you with an alibi for Friday afternoon. I have a God-fearing prick of an FBI agent with whom I have been trying to contend, and I have a lieutenant who can only wonder, *Why here in Putnam Landing?* Now, for Christ's sake, will you please calm down and be civil?"

With that, Sylvia became demure, saying, "I'm sorry, Gabe. I don't know what comes over me at times." She led Gabe into the living room and told him to sit down and that she would be right back. She disappeared toward the kitchen, returning in a few minutes with her drink refreshed. She sat beside Gabe on the sofa, curling one leg under her. She lit a Philip Morris, took a sip of the gin and tonic, and said, "I just need someone, someone to be near, someone to talk with. Don't you understand that, Gabe?"

Gabe didn't. He was the product of a harsh home environment. His mother was a soft, loving woman who nurtured, comforted, and loved his father, a harsh, alcoholic steelworker who was the exact opposite of his mother. Gabe was thirteen when his father, in a drunken stupor, discovered him crying in his bedroom while grieving his mother's death. He beat him, screaming that real men don't cry, not ever. Gabe's remaining years with him were difficult. The only support that Gabe ever received was for playing high school football. Considering that his father showed up for every game drunk, he was an obnoxious embarrassment for Gabe. So when he was found floating in the Elk Eye, just off the dock at Tim's Bar and Grill when Gabe was nineteen, Gabe never shed a tear. It was deemed that he was drunk and fell from the dock and drowned. Gabe never pursued it further, nor did the police.

Gabe, feeling uncomfortable with Sylvia's statement, quickly changed the subject. "When will the funeral be?"

She looked at him and snapped. "Christ, I need to talk, and all you can do is ask about Zane's funeral."

"Sylvia, I'm not sure what I have to offer. The only thing I can say is those kids need to be here with their mother for support and comfort at whatever level you can offer." Gabe recalled his mother's death, the total lack of support from his father, and how he had just watched his father crawl into a bottle and never come out.

"Brad and Caroline will be fine, damn it," she said. "I'm the one who needs to figure this whole marriage and life with Zane out so that I can better talk to my kids. The funeral is going to be on Monday at eleven o'clock for your information. He's going to be cremated. That's what he wanted, so it's the least I can do for him."

"Cremated? Has the body been released? Has the autopsy been completed?"

"All I know is that when I stopped at the Hillis Funeral Home after I left the lawyer, they told me that his body had been released and that it was on its way to Columbus for cremation."

"I haven't heard that. Who the hell gave permission for that?"

"I don't know, Gabe. I only know what I was told by the lawyer and by the Hills staff—that the body had been released for burial. Some Agent Matthews had approved it."

"Agent Matthews? Chester Matthews, that son of a bitch. He's circumventing me in the whole process again. I have to get back to the office to find out what the hell is going on." With that, Sylvia leaned over and planted a deep, wet kiss on Gabe's mouth. "No, no, this has to stop," he said. But Sylvia was beyond that. She stood up in front of him and removed her blouse and bra, exposing two perfectly formed, pink-tipped orbs. Her skirt fell to the floor, and she peeled her panties down her legs and stepped out of them, leaving nothing but her dark hose and garter belt. She then dropped to her knees before him and unfastened his belt and his pants, tugging them down around his ankles. She engulfed his half-hard member in her mouth. Gabe felt her soft lips and warm mouth going up and down on his cock, and he stopped her just in time. She rose from her knees and straddled him, guiding his erect penis into her sweet spot, as he had always called it. Their session lasted several minutes before Gabe exploded into her, and she followed him into ecstasy.

"God, Sylvia. You are so good. What was wrong with Zane for straying from this?" he said as she was climbing off him. "Look at that." He looked down at his limp, wet penis. "How can I go back to the station with this? I smell like a client in a whorehouse, sticky and smelly."

She dropped to her knees and again took his soft manhood, licking it, cleaning it for him. "Now you will be fine until you can get home for a shower."

"What do you mean, Sylvia? I feel like a wet noodle. I don't think I'll move again," was all he could manage to say.

"Fine then. You can just stay here with me. We'll fuck the rest of the day and all night, and I'll fix you a big breakfast in the morning."

With that, he stood up and dressed. "No—for God's sakes, that's all I need is for my car to be seen here in the morning. I have to go." Sylvia had not bothered to put her clothes on, and Gabe grabbed her, kissing her hard while fondling her right breast and nipple. She once again began to respond to his touch, but he released her, saying, "I have to go."

"Will you come back soon?" she asked.

"Yes, somehow, someway, I'll be back." Gabe knew that he was committing professional suicide by continuing this affair, but it was beyond his control. He knew that he would return to Sylvia.

As he left Northgate and pulled into the traffic, the thought flashed through his mind that he had not worn any protection.

As Gabe drove toward the station, Betty called him on the radio. "Yeah, Betty, go ahead."

"We located an address for Ernie Cobb, and he had priors in Cleveland, Dayton, and Indianapolis, also Illinois where he served time for rape."

"Why are you talking about him in the past tense?"

"Because we found his body on the back porch of his house on 327 Adams Street."

"His body?" Gabe responded. "Tell me he didn't die from old age."

"No, lead poisoning. Two to the head."

"Oh jeez, when did this happen?"

"Not sure, possibly yesterday."

"Okay, I'm on my way in. I'll be there in a few minutes."

What Gabe and nobody else in Putnam Landing knew was that a Russian operative was in town. Diane Smith, or Deidra Schmidt, on what was to be her last radio transmission to Moscow Central, had given Cobb's name and address as a potential threat to her cover. Moscow Central had taken this threat quite seriously and had provided this information to Yuri Gregorov to eliminate him along with Dr. Marchenko. Gregorov, posing as a federal agent, got into Cobb's rented house under the pretense of talking about Diane Smith and her work at Winston Optics. Cobb said that due to a lack of space in his refrigerator, he kept a cooler on the back porch with beer. He offered Gregorov a beer, which Yuri accepted, and as Ernie walked to the back porch, Yuri pulled out his Makarov 9 mm automatic with a silencer and shot Cobb twice in the back of the head. He fell dead to the porch floor, never knowing what hit him. Gregorov calmly walked to his car and drove away.

When Gabe arrived at the station, he met with the lieutenant, who filled him in on the latest murder. "Dr. Eli has the body, and we'll have more information after the autopsy. Do you think this is connected to the other murders?" Roy asked.

"Absolutely," Gabe said. "This guy was seen getting a blow job by Diane Smith by another employee, and he now winds up dead? What do you think, Roy?"

"I don't know. This whole thing has me perplexed. Why here? Why in this sleepy little town?"

"Roy, for fuck's sake, I don't know why. I just know that it's in our lap. We have to deal with it. We have to get to the bottom of this. I don't like it one bit better than you do, but it's ours, and we have to solve it, so let's get moving. Ernie Cobb must have found out something about Smith and presented a problem for her. She must have used that radio and told them—whoever *them* is. The KGB, army intelligence, and Moscow very likely sent someone to take care of the problem, and I believe Marchenko as well. That means that somewhere in Putnam Landing, we have a Russian assassin, and his next target is, without a doubt, Dr. Marchenko."

Gabe brought Lieutenant George up to speed about his interview with the scientist, finishing by saying, "There's something going on here, Roy, and I believe that physicist is in danger."

"Shouldn't we provide protection for him? Maybe a couple of plain clothes to tag him for a while."

"If I can spare the men, that's a good idea. Just tell them not to be made," Gabe said.

"Well, I'll get on that right away," George said. "But first, I've got to see that damn reporter from the *Democrat*. What's her name, Rosemary, Rose, something? You know her, don't you, Gabe?"

"Her name is Rosary Benedict," Gabe answered.

"Oh yeah, that's it. Named after the beads. Jesus, why would anyone name a kid that?"

"Good Catholics, Roy, but possibly a bit too much with that name."

"Gabe, you know her. You've been out with her. Why don't you—"

"No way, Roy. She's yours, and that's your job. You talk to her. Just don't give her too much," Gabe snapped. "I'm going to Eli's office to talk about the autopsies. I'll see you tomorrow."

"Well, shit, Gabe, send her in on your way out," said the lieutenant.

"Okay, I will—and good luck." Gabe smiled, then left the office and encountered Rosary Benedict in the waiting room.

She immediately accosted Gabe, saying, "Gabe, what can you tell about this most recent killing of Ernest Cobb? Is his murder connected to Zane Winston and his mistress?"

"Rose, the lieutenant will answer all your questions. He's waiting for you in his office. Go through that door, and you'll find him," he said as he gently took her elbow and guided her through the door into the detective room.

Lieutenant George was right. Detective St. John knew Rosary Benedict. He had picked her up one night at Tim's Bar and Grill. She was very drunk, and they had spent a fun night in the back seat of his car. When he took her home at daylight, he asked to see her again, and she had replied, "Tonight." When he knocked on her door that night, she opened the door and pulled him inside her apartment. Gabe did not leave her apartment until Sunday evening. All during their session, she kept asking him to convert to Catholicism, and he kept telling her that he was a Catholic. By Sunday afternoon, Gabe was agreeing to anything, and Rosary kept on converting. She, however, missed Mass on Sunday morning. Gabe figured that proselytizing for the faith must give her a special dispensation. Gabe remembered all of this as he drove across the bridge over the Elk Eye on his way to Dr. Mason's house and office.

As he pulled up in front of the house, he saw no cars. Must be a light day for *Eli*, he thought. He went into the office but saw no one. Betty's desk was empty, so he thought she must have left for the day. Gabe then heard muffled voices coming from upstairs. Gabe knew that Dr. Mason had converted one of the original bedrooms into a study library. He had spent several enjoyable evenings with Eli there, drinking quality bourbon and smoking fine cigars. Gabe began to ascend the stairs. About halfway up, he found a woman's blouse lying as though it had been quickly discarded. As he proceeded to the top of the steps, he found a bra. Looking at the size, he read 36D. *Wow*, he thought, *that's a woman.* Hearing muffled voices coming from the study, he cautiously proceeded to open the door. There he found Ms. Shaw seated in his large armchair, with Eli nude from the waist up, on his knees between her legs, with his head buried in her lap. Gabe watched for a few seconds, then discretely backed out of the room and retreated to the steps, where he waited for them to finish. When he heard Ms. Shaw's moans of release and ecstasy, he called, "Eli, Eli, are you up here?"

With that, he heard them scrambling in the study.

Gabe loudly said, "Eli, it's me, Gabe. I need to talk with you."

"No problem, Gabe. I'm just giving some dictation to Ms. Shaw. I'll be with you in a minute."

"Oh, that's fine," Gabe responded, chuckling to himself about the dictation. A few seconds later, Ms. Shaw emerged from the study wearing a bathrobe, saying, "I spilled coffee on the front of me, so I had to put this on." She glanced down to the floor where her bra was lying.

"Those things happen, Ms. Shaw. I just need some time with Dr. Mason."

"Well, go right in. We just finished, and I'll be going home now." She proceeded down the stairs in her signature high heels.

Gabe entered Eli's study, saying, "Hello, and good to be in here again." Eli reciprocated the salutation and offered the detective a bourbon. He looked at his watch and said, "Okay, Eli, close enough. Let's have one."

Eli poured two bourbons over ice, and the two men settled into the comfortable surroundings of the study. They both lit cigarettes as Gabe asked the coroner about the autopsies on Diane Smith and Zane Winston. "Well, I sent that report to the lieutenant, Gabe, and it's pretty much as I told you at the scene; it was a professional hit. There were two shooters, one for Zane and another for the girl. They both were shot with a .38 Special, hollow points. I was able to recover enough of both slugs from the bodies to reliably confirm two killers. I would say that one or both of them had powerful enemies who were sent from out of town to make the hit."

"What can you tell me about the girl, Diane Smith? You said you had seen her as a patient several months ago here in the office?"

Dr. Mason hesitated. "Now, Gabe, you know the process. You subpoena me, I appear in court, the judge grants me immunity, and then I can answer questions."

"Horseshit, Eli. You and I have been friends and worked together for too long for you not to talk to me on the QT. You should know that whatever you say to me, or whatever I possibly uncovered about you and Ms. Shaw, will be held in the utmost confidence."

The doctor took a drag on his cigarette and sipped his bourbon, looking at the detective. "Blackmail is such an ugly word, Gabriel. I am shocked that you have sunk to this."

"Oh, Eli, I don't give a damn about what you and Ms. Shaw are doing, and your secret is safe with me, but I'm getting desperate. I think the killers are either returning to Putnam Landing or they may be here already. I believe their job wasn't finished."

"What do you mean? Who else is there?"

"I have to know whatever I tell you will be held in absolute confidence. You know, Doc, patient-doctor stuff."

"Okay, Gabe, I get the point. I saw Diane Smith last winter, as I told you at the scene. I treated her for a bad yeast infection, and that's really it. In the autopsy report, however, I note that sometime in her past she delivered a baby."

"Oh my gosh. Zane's?"

"No, probably ten to fifteen years ago when she was much younger."

"Wow," Gabe responded, mouth agape. "What do you suppose happened to it?"

"I have no idea. I can only report what I find medically, but she has definitely given birth. It's up to you to figure out the rest."

"Well, Doc, what's with you and Ms. Shaw?" Gabe questioned.

"Gabriel, some things are better left unsaid, and I believe this is one of those. And now, if you're finished with your bourbon …"

"Oh yeah, sure, Eli, I'll just be going now. Thanks for your time, and I'll be in touch with you."

"Quite all right, Gabe. Anytime I can help you, don't hesitate—but call first, okay?"

"Okay, Doc." Gabe laughed. "And thanks again."

Gabe left the study and went down the steps. When he got to the bottom of the wide stairway, he glanced toward Ms. Shaw's desk. It was empty, but as he stepped through the large front door under the porch, he noticed Betty Shaw's Chevrolet sitting in her parking place. *Doc, you old dog,* he thought with a smile.

On his way home, he stopped at the West View Grill for a pack of cigarettes, where he encountered Eloise Fletcher. As they both were leaving, Gabe suggested that she follow him home, and she readily agreed.

The two assassins had tracked Victor Marchenko during the week. They knew when he arrived at work and when he went home. They knew the schedule of the household, when his housekeeper came and when she left. They just needed to arrive at the best time and place to make the hit and get out of the city.

After watching him all week, they discovered that Marchenko left the lab earlier on Friday's. With this in mind, they decided to hit him on the ensuing Friday.

The hill above Linden Avenue was heavily wooded and would provide adequate cover for a shooter. The distance from there to the parking lot of Winston Optics was approximately two hundred yards, an easy shot for Carl.

Detective St. John attended Zane Winston's funeral on Monday. Monsignor Murphy praised Zane for being a stalwart member of the parish and the community, as well as being a wonderful husband and father. Gabe chuckled to himself, thinking, *If you only knew, Monsignor.* He then caught himself and thought, *He knows.* He knew all too well.

Sylvia looked stunning, dressed in a muted-green suit with black leather heels. Her two children appeared to be forlorn and confused about Zane's death. Gabe suspected that they had received very little support or understanding from their mother. She was too busy hitting the liquor bottle to even notice them. He had pangs of sorrow as he remembered his own mother's death. He quickly shook those feelings off as he scanned the congregation for a strange face, a face that didn't fit in Putnam Landing. He saw no one who did not appear to belong. It was the usual coming together of friends and relatives, most of whom Gabe recognized or knew.

It was a hot June day, and Gabe began to perspire profusely. He became aware of the .38 Super sheathed in the leather shoulder holster. Under that holster, it felt like it was a hundred degrees. *Damn*, he thought, *why didn't I carry my Model 10 snub nose?* The Model 10 was department issue and the pistol that all the detectives were to carry, but Gabe liked a little more hitting power, so he purchased the Smith & Wesson automatic and .38 Super. It was loaded with hollow-point ammunition, another no-no within the department. Gabe, however, felt more secure with their stopping power. The automatic was a heavier pistol, and at the moment, he wished he had carried the revolver in his belt holster. He came back to reality when he heard Monsignor Murphy saying, "The mass has ended. Go in peace." He remained in his seat, awaiting further instructions from the undertaker for the procession to the cemetery.

It was then that Gabe saw him—a tall, well-built, well-dressed man who was out of his pew and walking across the aisle toward the pew where Dr. Marchenko had been sitting. Victor Marchenko was just exiting Holy Rosary Catholic Church at the direction of the undertaker when Gabe reacted. He leapt from the pew and ran, dodging the people lining up to exit. By the time he arrived at the exit, he saw Yuri Gregorov's automatic pistol. Gabe pushed two people to the sidewalk as he drew his gun and yelled, "Police! Drop your weapon now!" Funeral attendees began screaming and trying to get out of the way. Gregorov spun to face the detective with his Makarov leveled at Gabe and with his finger on the trigger. But before he could shoot, Gabe fired twice from his .38 Super; both of his hollow-point rounds struck Yuri in the upper chest, tearing two holes through him. The Russian fell, dead. Screaming funeral attendees scattered in all directions as Gabe approached the body on the sidewalk. He kicked the Makarov away and secured Dr. Marchenko in his car, telling him to lie down on the back seat and telling the driver to take him to the police station PDQ and get him inside.

The driver started the engine and left immediately. He pulled out his own pistol as he proceeded down Main Street to the police station.

Father Bennett, the assistant priest at Holy Rosary, was busy administering the last rites to the dead man. In a matter of moments, police swarmed the church. Most of the funeral procession had already left before the shooting started, and Zane got buried on time, albeit with only about half the mourners.

The next morning, Atherton was up early and went down to the motel coffee shop for breakfast. When he passed through the motel lobby on his way to breakfast, he stopped to purchase a copy of the *Democrat*. He received his coffee and placed his breakfast order with the attractive young waitress. He then began perusing the newspaper. Atherton's eyes fixated on the headline "Heroic Cop Stops Murder Attempt, Shoots Suspect." By the time he had finished reading about the shooting incident and the dead John Doe at Holy Rosary Catholic Church, Carl made his appearance.

"Anything exciting happening in this sleepy burg?" he sarcastically asked of Thomas.

"Nothing more than the death of our Russian friend at the church at Zane Winston's funeral yesterday," Atherton responded.

"What? You've gotta be kidding me."

"Not in the least, Carl. The Russian was shot dead by this cop, Gabriel St. John. I think we better be on the lookout for this guy. We don't want him throwing a monkey wrench into the works, and he very well could. We need to watch him."

Carl thought for a moment and then said, "Do we need to tail him too?"

"I think that we'll need to know where he is on Friday afternoon. I don't want any fuckups this time. Tell you what—you shadow the cop this week, and I'll stay with Marchenko. Then on Friday, we'll make the hit and get out of town."

"Sounds like a plan, Thomas," Waters responded as the waitress brought their breakfast. "At a funeral, in church—are you serious?"

Atherton shrugged and began eating.

Monday morning arrived too early for Carl Waters. He had spent most of Sunday night in his motel room with a bottle of bourbon, which he had managed to deplete by the time he fell asleep in the chair. When Atherton aroused him at six o'clock in the morning, it was a chore. "goddamn it, Carl. This job needs you to be at your best, not in a drunken haze."

"I'm okay, Thomas. Honest, I am," he said as he struggled to get out of the armchair. "Honest, I'm fine. Just let me get a shower and revive myself."

Atherton, shaking his head, replied, "Get with it, Goddamn it. You need to be at the police station."

"I know, I know, and I will be. I'll be there by six thirty. Don't worry," Carl said as he slowly moved toward the bathroom.

Oh God, Thomas thought, *maybe it's worth it if it gets him into the shower and clean clothes.* He almost chuckled to himself as he said that, but given the seriousness of their mission, he could not allow himself that luxury. Carl emerged from the shower fifteen minutes later, and Thomas emphatically stated, "Clean clothes, Carl. Not those same shit-stained underwear and smelly pants you've been wearing all week."

"Jesus, you're worse than my mother," he said, searching his duffel for clean clothes.

When he was dressed, he headed for the restaurant for a carryout coffee before setting out for the police station.

At eight thirty, Carl, armed with Gabe's picture from the newspaper, recognized him going into the station. He also saw Agent Chester Matthews entering the station. Not that Carl knew Agent Matthews, but he knew the type—clean-cut, dressed in a dark suit, wearing a white shirt with a dark tie and wing tips. *There goes a Feebie*, he thought.

Inside the station, Agent Matthews was conducting the meeting with Detective St. John, Lieutenant George, and Chief Cochran. "Wow, you guys have had a busy weekend," Agent Matthews began. "Nice work, Detective. Good shot and no civilians injured. That's the best part. These things can get real messy when bystanders get hurt or killed. The Bureau certainly appreciates your judicious use of force and accurate shooting."

Gabe St. John didn't give a good Goddamn what the Bureau appreciated. He just wanted good information to help solve the case.

Chief Cochran said, "I just can't believe that they, he, whoever, would choose to make a kill at Holy Rosary Church during a funeral. Good heavens, it's packed with people attending the funeral mass. It just doesn't make any sense. A hundred people as witnesses."

"Chief," Agent Matthews said, "I agree with that to a point, but once the shooting starts and the mark falls, people are engaged in panic. All they care about is saving themselves, and the shooter calmly walks away from the mayhem he created. No two witnesses' statements are the same. He was tall, he was short, he was dark, he was light. Law enforcement is left with no solid information, and the perp gets out of town. They're well trained for this type of scenario."

"Who's well trained for this type of scenario, Chet?" Gabe asked.

"Agents of the Soviet KGB." The agent watched as all three of the men's jaws dropped.

"Are you saying this guy was the hit man for the KGB?" Gabe exclaimed. Even though Gabe had had his suspicions that there was an assassin in Putnam Landing, to hear it boldly confirmed was a shock.

"Yes," Agent Matthews responded, "not just an agent. One of their very best. Moscow wants Victor Marchenko dead. He is Russian born, you know, and if they can't have him back, they want him eliminated so that he cannot contribute to our missile development. More than likely, he also killed that Cobb fellow. Cobb was probably getting close to Diane Smith and could have been about to blow her cover. Director Hoover has taken a very special interest in this case." St. John expected Matthews to genuflect at the mention of Hoover's name, but the agent continued standing as he went on talking. "He has made calls and arranged meetings to try to get to the bottom of this situation, and I must say what he has been able to find out is more than helpful to us and our case."

Gabe smirked, thinking, *That old queer. He knows who's sucking whose cock in Washington and has probably threatened to make this public if he didn't get answers.*

"Our director, through a deep-covered source inside the CIA, was able to obtain a complete dossier on our shooter. He was Yuri Gregorov, born in Stalingrad and there during the war when the Wehrmacht lay siege to the city. Apparently, he saw his entire family killed by the Germans in one way or another. He got hold of a sniper's rifle and began killing Germans to even the score. This brought him to the attention of Moscow Station, who saw potential in his raw abilities. They whisked him out of Stalingrad after the Germans surrendered and sent him to Moscow. He spent the next five years undergoing intensive training, first by the NKBD and then the KGB in weapons, psychology, martial arts, and language. He was a loner and worked alone on his assignments. We can attribute several assassinations to him in the Caribbean, South America, and Asia. We also know that he is a German hater, given his background. So this Deidra Schmidt may have been on his list as well."

"Hold on, Chet. We've got two shooters for her, documented by the autopsy. Is there another Russian running around Putnam Landing?"

"Let's not get ahead of ourselves, Gabe. We also discovered that there is very likely a CIA team here intent on killing Marchenko."

"What in the hell are you saying, Chet? Are you saying that our own government wants this guy dead too?"

"Apparently," Matthews continued, "it seems that a department within the CIA specializing in that work has sent a two-man team to take out Victor Marchenko."

"What the hell for?" Gabe inquired. "He's on our side. He's working for us, isn't he?"

"They seem to think that he and Deidra were in cahoots and spying for the Russians," Agent Matthews said.

Gabe continued, "You're telling me that we have, right here in Putnam Landing, two CIA operatives who are in town to kill Dr. Marchenko?"

"That's what I'm telling you. The man is in mortal danger, and I cannot help you with the protection."

"What in the hell are you telling us? We have a man living amongst us who is in danger of being assassinated, and the Goddamn FBI won't help protect him?"

"My hands are tied. I cannot protect an enemy of the state. I have been ordered to stand down."

"Stand down? Stand down? What in the fuck are you talking about? You're going to watch a helpless old scientist be murdered because you've been told to stand down?"

"Gabe, my hands are tied. I have been ordered to do nothing, to not interfere in any way."

"Chet, how can you say this? That Goddamn CIA is not supposed to be working on American soil. That's *your* responsibility. Now, what in the hell is going on?"

"I don't know, Gabe. I just have my orders."

"Well, Chet, your orders suck—and even you know that!" Gabe yelled.

"Detective St. John, will you be quiet and let Agent Matthews finish his report for us?" Lieutenant George said, glaring at Gabe. Gabe leaned back in his chair, seething but silent.

Agent Matthews continued, "Now, for additional insight into Deidra Schmidt—or Diane Smith, as she was known here in Putnam Landing—from our CIA source, we have learned that she had two older brothers and a sister. They were all dead by the time Deidra was born. We're not sure how they died, but we suspect it was typhus. There was an outbreak in Baden-Baden around the time she was born, and that possibly was the reason for their move to Berlin. Anyway, Hitler, her father's death, war, and destruction, and her mother died when Deidra was young, probably in the hands of the Russians who took Berlin. She was carried to Moscow where she underwent state indoctrination and then trained for the NKBD, which became the KGB. We know that as a final part of her initiation into the spy organization, she was given to a horny old comrade where she was brutally beaten and repeatedly raped. Quite likely, that is the child she delivered, as mentioned in the autopsy report. She was active in Italy in '47 and in Greece in '49. She turned up at Ohio State University where she was awarded a graduate degree, and other than this, we have nothing more on Deidra Schmidt until she turned up in Putnam Landing several years ago."

"Agent Matthews, what about this Hungarian delegation that was visiting Winston Optics?" Lieutenant George asked.

"That delegation was just a benign group of Hungarian businessmen and industrialists who were visiting as much for goodwill as anything else. From what we can tell, there was one among them who was KGB, but whether or not he was able to meet with Deidra, we don't know."

"Well, we read in the paper that the group's interpreter, a Vacalov somebody, was found murdered in an alley in New York City a few days after they left Putnam Landing," Roy George continued.

"Vacalov was ours. We don't know if he was made by the Ruskies and taken out or if it was a random act of violence in New York City. That's still being investigated. Are there any other questions or concerns before I leave?" the agent asked as he gathered his material.

"I have a question for you, Chet," Gabe said, restraining his anger toward the FBI agent. Roy George cringed in his chair, while Chief Cochran stared blankly.

"Okay, Gabe, what is it?" the agent coldly responded.

"Could you please explain to me why our own government wants this man dead? I mean, he has been contributing to our military by developing guidance systems for our missiles, so why kill him?"

"Gabe, that's a fair question, and what I'm about to divulge to you must stay within this room. Victor Marchenko, as a Russian, is suspected to be in collusion with the spy, Deidra Schmidt."

"Oh, horseshit," Gabe said. "I talked to people at the plant, and no one liked that woman, especially Dr. Marchenko. He avoided her like the plague. He never let her into his laboratory at that plant. He flat out did not trust her. Now explain this—if he was collaborating with Diane

Smith and passing valuable national security information to the Soviets, then why would Moscow Station send an assassin to kill him?"

"Well, Gabe, there are some things in these cases that we just aren't supposed to know, and I believe that this must be one of those."

"Oh, horseshit," Gabe said. "It doesn't add up. You don't send a hit man from Moscow to kill a man who was spying for your country. I would say that he was not spying for the Soviets but is contributing to this country's military program, and that's why they want him dead. Now you had better send that message up through channels and get them to call off the hit on Dr. Marchenko."

"There is nothing I can do to stop this. Locally, the Bureau is not to be involved."

"Jesus Christ, Chet! You know that nothing about this adds up. You have got to do something to help us prevent an innocent man's death."

Agent Matthews cringed at Detective St. John's reference to the deity, responding, "Detective, there is nothing more I can do." With that, he walked out of the office.

As Gabe got up to leave, Lieutenant George stopped him and said, "Gabe, you were out of line."

"Out of line! That's horseshit, and you know it, Roy. Nothing about this whole thing adds up. Nothing. You're going to let an old man who's doing good things for our government get killed just because that pompous ass of an FBI agent says we have to. Well, goddamn it, I don't have to, and what's more, I'm not going to. If you won't authorize around-the-clock protection for him, then I'll do it myself. You can do whatever you want with me, but that's what I'm going to do, Roy." With that, Gabe left the office.

Betty met him as he exited with a stack of ten messages—two from Denise Potts, one from Olivia Rozane, one from Eloise Fletcher, and the rest from Sylvia Winston. *Olivia Rozane? Who the hell is that, and what the hell does she want?* he thought.

Atherton and Waters used the week traipsing the hill above Linden Avenue and the Winston Optic parking lot to find the prime location for a sniper to do his work. Carl found it. A young sassafras with a low branch that he could use to steady his rifle to make the shot. It was about two hundred yards. "Carl, can you make the hit from here?" Tommy asked.

"No problem. With this M1 sniper rifle, it'll be a chip shot." Carl had the entire CIA arsenal available to him, and he had selected the M1. "I used this baby in Europe during the war, and I know it. I am used to it. With this, I could hit the eye of a fly at this range."

"Okay, Carl, you're the shooter, and I rely on you to make the hit," Atherton said.

As they turned to walk the hundred yards back to the street where their car was parked, they encountered a man. He was obviously drunk and from the neighborhood. He asked, "What the hell are you fellows during here?"

"Well, we're just doing some hiking," Waters feebly responded.

"Hiking? Dressed up like this?"

"Yeah, well, we just wanted to see what was growing on this hill," Thomas quickly responded.

"Oh, well, okay, but dressed in a tie and a sport jacket. I guess then it takes all kinds," he said, turning away from Waters and walking back toward his house.

Carl drew his silenced revolver and fired one round, striking the neighbor in the back of the head. Atherton, who was in front of him, was covered with a bloody spray and pieces of the guy's brains. "Why in the hell did you do that?" Atherton said.

"The guy would have made us," was Carl's only reply.

"Jesus! What do we do with him now?" Thomas remarked as he looked at the dead body on the ground.

"We bury him and get the hell out of here."

Thirty minutes later, they had him buried well enough and were carefully walking to their car. "This is not good, Carl. He's going to be missed," Atherton stated as the two got into their car. "Someone is going to be looking for him, and they'll file a police report. Jesus! Why did you have to shoot him?"

"For once, Tommy boy, it was my call," Carl replied. "The bastard was drunk, and within in an hour, he would have had our presence in those woods broadcast all over that neighborhood. I summed up the situation and made the decision to eliminate a threat to our mission."

"Carl," Atherton said as he put the car in gear and started up Taylor Street, "there could have been another way."

"Tell me what, Tommy. Tell me what your way would have been."

"I don't fucking know, but I was thinking about it when you impulsively pulled the trigger."

"That's the trouble with you college boys—too much thinking, not enough action. If we had too many like you during the war, we would have lost it. We had to react quickly to stay alive."

"Carl, goddamn it, I understand that, but we are not behind the lines in France fighting a hot war anymore. We are fighting a cold war, and this war requires different tactics. Today, it's more like a chess game, plotting quiet strategy and gently executing it. It's not the Wild West where we go in with six-guns blazing."

"Tommy boy, I never was interested in the queer game—chess, that is. What I would do instead of moving pieces all over that board is shoot the king and grab that fucking queen and game over."

As they pulled into the parking lot of the motel, Atherton realized that this conversation was over and that they would just have to deal with it if there were consequences from Carl's actions.

Once they were inside their motel room, Atherton quickly stripped off his clothes and placed them in a pile on the floor by his bed, then disappeared into the bathroom for a hot shower. When he returned to the room, he observed Carl sullenly drinking bourbon over a little ice. He decided he had better approach him before that got too far out of hand. As he dried off and began dressing, he said to Carl, "You know, I've been thinking—"

"Oh, fucking wonderful. The college boy has been thinking," Carl interrupted.

Atherton had had enough of this oaf for one day. He looked at Waters and said, "Carl, shut the fuck up. I have had it with you and your complete fuckups. We're going to change your location of the shot to that old water tower on the hill. You compromised the other spot, so we're changing locations, and Goddamn it, that's the way it is. We'll go tomorrow on the rutted dirt road behind the tank, and you can figure out the shot, and maybe we won't be seen or noticed."

Carl, who had just enough alcohol to make him mellow, replied, "Okay, Thomas, I'll make that work."

By eight o'clock the next morning, the two assassins were traversing the bulldozed and rutted road through what had once been a prosperous farm field. The land had been purchased by a developer who was in the process of laying the farm out into housing plots. The road was only a temporary access for the contractor and his crews. The morning was quiet with no signs of activity anywhere. Atherton and Waters walked to the old water tower on the edge of the hill overlooking Linden Avenue and the Winston plant. The water tank had been used by the Putnam Landing Tile Company to produce their world-famous tile used by both home and industry. The tank was no longer in use and was falling into a state of disrepair, with water leaking out of it and the wooden structure beginning to decay. When the two assassins had first seen it, they thought it had potential as the place to take the shot. Carl, however, nixed the idea after climbing up the wooden ladder, breaking off two steps as he climbed to the catwalk. "No way," he said. "This thing is about to fall over. We need another site for the shot." But now, given Carl's impetuous shooting of the civilian, it was the spot.

"Be careful ascending the ladder, Carl," Atherton said to Waters as he began climbing.

"It isn't just the Goddamn ladder, Thomas. It's the catwalk as well. The boards are rotten, and some are missing, and the water constantly running out of this tank is a constant distraction."

Atherton understood but replied, "During the war, I'm sure you had many difficult shots, but you still were successful. You still made the shot and completed your mission."

"I know, I know, Thomas," Carl responded, "but that was a long time ago, and I was younger."

"Oh, horseshit, Carl. Get on with it," was Atherton's stern reply.

"Okay, okay, I'm on it." Carl climbed the ladder to the catwalk. He gingerly proceeded to the front of the water tank and viewed the street below and the plant. He estimated about 250 yards for the shot. The rail in front of the water tower surrounding the catwalk appeared to be sturdy enough to support the M1 rifle. He commented, "It's a long shot. I'd say 200 to 275, but it's possible. I can make it."

Atherton replied, "Okay, come on down. You have three days to think about it."

Carl descended to the ground and said, "I can make the shot, Thomas. Don't worry."

Atherton merely nodded.

As they left the water tower, on the edge of the wooded hill, they heard loud voices. They appeared to be young boys across the road in the woods overlooking Military Road, which led down to Linden Avenue. They were arguing about how to build something, a cabin, a tree house. Atherton said, "Don't shoot them, Carl," as he drove the car slowly down the rutted hill toward Military Road and onto Linden Avenue.

Detective St. John slept in until almost nine o'clock, but he was not alone. Lying next to him was the reporter, Rosary Benedict. He had found her waiting for him on his porch steps when he arrived home the previous evening. She was sitting facing the sidewalk with her knees slightly apart for Gabe's benefit, and he did not let that go unnoticed as he approached her. "Rose, what are you doing here?"

She stood up, saying, "I need to talk with you about the shooting at Holy Rosary. What the hell is going on?"

"What, what do you mean? There's nothing going on, Rose. Just some nutcase at the funeral with a gun who was trying to shoot Dr. Marchenko."

"You mean the scientist from Winston Optics?"

"Yes, that's the one," Gabe replied.

"But why, Gabe? Why would anyone want to kill him? What has he done to anybody?"

"We don't know, but we're working on that," Gabe nonchalantly commented as he unlocked his door and stepped inside, hoping Rosary would leave. She didn't. She pushed in behind him, entering the house. "Come on, Rose. I can't tell you any more, and I'm tired. It's been a long day." He glanced over Rosary's shoulder and caught a glimpse of Eloise Fletcher's car driving slowly past his house. *What's she doing here?* he thought as he quickly closed the front door.

He went into the living room, dropping his sports jacket, necktie, and shoulder holster on the large chair. He then stepped out of his loafers and walked to the kitchen. "Do you want a drink, Rose?" he yelled to her.

"Sure, that would be nice," came her response.

Gabe cut two pieces of lemon, filled the glasses with ice, gin, and a splash of tonic, and reentered the living room. Rosary had removed her shoes and was sitting with her legs curled up under her on the couch. She lit a cigarette as Gabe set the drinks on the coffee table. As he dropped down beside her, he became aware of her faint perfume and body scent while lighting his cigarette.

"Well, Gabe, what was this shooter's name? We don't have anything at the paper."

"Then you have as much as we have. We don't know anything about him. As far as a name, we have him listed as John Doe. He had nothing on him to identify who he was or where he came from. We're just at a standstill."

"Well, what about Ernie Cobb on Adams Street? Are these two related? I mean did the John Doe and Cobb know each other?"

"I don't think so. There's nothing in our investigation that links the two in any way," Gabe lied as he stubbed out his Chesterfield in the ashtray. Rosary uncoiled her legs from under her and repositioned her body on the couch so that her back was now propped against two pillows on the arm of the couch. This provided Gabe with a view of her long legs, to the top of her garter belt and the silk triangle between her thighs.

From there on, the evening and night became a blur until nine o'clock the next morning when Gabe was aroused once more by Rosary's mouth on his penis. She then got out of bed, showered, dressed, and with a parting kiss said, "You owe me this story, Gabe, and I want it! I need it!"

Gabe showered and dressed, then headed for Kate's where, for once, he did not refuse her full breakfast. He devoured every bit of it and followed it with several cups of Kate's strong coffee and several Chesterfields. It was well after ten o'clock by the time Gabe entered the station. Betty greeted him with several messages from Sylvia, another from Olivia Rozane, and one from Rosary Benedict, simply saying, "Thanks for last night." *Oh shit,* he thought. But looking at Betty, her smile said it all, so he made no reply. There was also one from Eloise Fletcher, and this one disturbed him. As he entered the detective's room, he met Lieutenant George.

"Morning, Roy," Gabe said.

"Morning?" Roy George replied. "Well, it may be morning to some but not to me or anyone else who has to work for a living."

"Take it easy. I needed to rest up a bit."

"Yeah, well, don't we all. And don't make this a habit, Gabe. You know, taxpayers and all of that. I wanted to tell you that Chief Cochran authorized two blues to be with Dr. Marchenko from six in the morning until ten o'clock at night. That's the best I could get from him in light of what Chester Matthews said."

"Well, I guess that's better than nothing, but, Jesus, what about from ten until six in the morning?"

"I know, Gabe, but that's it. That's the best I could do."

"Okay, Roy. That's better than nothing. I'll take it," Gabe said. "Can you help me with a name? Olivia Rozane. She's called me twice, and I can't figure out who she is or what she wants."

"Olivia Rozane," Roy said, and then it came to him. "She's old George Rozane's widow, the millionaire pottery magnate's wife. She lives next door to where Zane Winston was killed."

"Oh, yeah, okay. I know exactly where she lives. I'm going there right away."

"Just get this thing solved, Gabe," the lieutenant replied. "I'm starting to feel the pressure."

Gabe left the station and headed for the Maple Place address next to the murdered girl's apartment. He pulled into the driveway of the Rozane mansion underneath the large carport on the left side of the house. He decided he had better not park his car there. The spot was reserved for the household. He coasted the car out from under the carport toward the back of the driveway. Stepping out of the car, he began to approach the side entrance into the house from the carport. Once again, he halted, thinking, *These people would expect a visitor to use the front door. It may be more proper.* So, with a shrug, he went around to the large front door and rang the doorbell.

Gabe waited for a few seconds for the door to swing open. An older woman, tall, erect, and well dressed in a black suit with a stiff white blouse, stood in the doorway. "Yes, how can I help you, young man? If you are a salesman, please go to the back door and ask for Ms. Gillogly." Her graying hair was pulled tightly to the back of her head, and she was wearing wire-rimmed glasses on the end of her nose. As she spoke, she cocked her head so that it appeared that she was looking down on Gabe. She reminded Gabe of the hens that his father kept in the backyard when he was a kid, only more ominous.

"Ma'am, I'm not selling anything. I'm Detective Gabriel St. John with Putnam Landing Police." He pulled out his badge to confirm his identity. "I'm here to see Mrs. Olivia Rozane. Are you she?"

"Sir, I am not. I am Ms. Evelyn Snead, housekeeper to the Rozane household for thirty-six years. Now, young man, why do you want to see Mrs. Rozane?" Ms. Snead spoke these last words with a certain amount of disdain for the policeman standing before her.

"Ms. Snide, is it?"

"Snead."

"Oh, yes," Gabe replied. "I have no idea why I'm here. It was your *employer* who contacted me. Now I'm here to find out how I can help her and why she contacted me. Will you please let her know that I'm standing on the front porch?"

Evelyn Snead's demeanor softened a bit as she asked, "Is it about that messy business next door with that tramp?"

"I don't know. That's what I'm here to find out."

"Oh, yes, of course, please." She motioned for Gabe to step into the house. "Come in." As he stepped into the large hall, he noticed the elevator in the back of the hall near the wide staircase. Ms. Snead said, "Ms. Rozane is in her upstairs sitting room. Detective, please follow me." And with that, Evelyn Snead led the way up the gently curving stairs to the second floor of the house. Gabe noticed five doors at the top of the stairs, three of which were opened into bedrooms. There were two closed, and the housekeeper approached one and knocked softly on the door. She proceeded to open it and announced, "Detective Gabriel St. John to see you, Madam."

Gabe followed her into the room, which was large with a fireplace. There was a daybed against one wall and bookcases lining the opposing wall. The room was painted in a hunter green with photographs hanging everywhere. A small, short, gray-haired, thin woman, dressed in slacks and a blouse, rose from her large credenza in front of the windows. The woman's large, sparkling blue eyes and rather sharp facial features reminded Gabe of a fox. "Detective," she said in her raspy voice, "thank you so much for making time in your busy day to call on me."

"Well, ma'am, you requested to see me, so I thought I had better stop by."

"I am so glad you did. Can I offer you something, coffee, tea, or something a bit stronger?"

"Well, ma'am, coffee wound be fine, if it's not too much trouble."

"No trouble at all, Detective St. John. Evelyn, please bring us coffee."

"Yes, ma'am. I shall bring it up."

"Thank you," Olivia Rozane said to the housekeeper. "Please get it now." The housekeeper left the room closing the door behind her.

"Now, Detective, the reason for my calls to you," Olivia said as she lit a Camel cigarette and sat down in a large wing chair across from the sofa where she motioned for Gabe to sit. As he sat down, he felt as though he might sink to the first floor below. The eiderdown cushions were softer and more comfortable than anything he had ever experienced. Olivia offered him a cigarette.

"Thank you, Mrs. Rozane. I'm just about out of mine, so thank you," he said.

"Help yourself, Detective." She pushed the Royal Doulton cigarette box across the coffee table in his direction.

"Thank you, ma'am."

"And please," Olivia Rozane said before taking a deep drag of her cigarette, "call me Olivia."

"Well, yes, ma'am, okay, Olivia," Gabe stammered out. "How can I help you, Olivia?"

"Detective, what do you go by? Gabriel, Gabe, what?"

"Gabe."

"Okay, Gabe. Well, on the day that simple Zane and that poor girl were killed, I was in the bathroom taking a shower. When I finished my shower and was drying, I glanced out of the window, and there they were."

"Who?" Gabe asked.

"Well, what do you mean, Gabe?" she asked. "Those two murderers! That's who!"

"Are you telling me that you saw two men shoot Zane Winston and Diane Smith?"

"Well, not actually shoot them," Olivia Rozane stated as she lit another Camel. "But it's the same as shooting them. I mean I saw them leaving her apartment. You're the detective. Can't you put it together from here?"

"Olivia, you are an eyewitness, our only eyewitness. Can you describe these men? What time of day was it? Where did they go? What kind of car were they driving?"

She took a drag on her cigarette and began to respond as the sitting room door opened and Ms. Snead entered carrying a tray of coffee and cups. The fresh brewed coffee emitted a wonderful aroma, and Gabe lit another Chesterfield in anticipation of tasting the brew. Ms. Snead sat the tray on the coffee table and began to fill the cups. She hesitated a moment to ask Gabe if he used sugar or cream. Gabe shook his head while answering, "No, I don't spoil good coffee, and that smells wonderful, Ms. Snead."

"Thank you." Ms. Snead continued filling the cups, serving Olivia first and then the detective.

Olivia pointedly said to the housekeeper, "Thank you, Evelyn. I will take care of it from here. That will be all." Ms. Snead turned and left the room, closing the heavy door with a noticeable thud. Olivia shook her head and commented, "That woman is wonderful at running the house, but there are those times when she's a pain in the ass."

"I think I might know what you're saying," Gabe responded with a slight grin, remembering what it took for him just to get into the house. "But tell me more about the two men you observed from the window," he said, then sipped the coffee and continued smoking his last Chesterfield.

"There were two, both in their late thirties or early forties. One tall, thin, and nicely dressed. The other one shorter, stouter, and barrel-chested." Gabe nodded, and she continued. "They were on that small porch closing the door to the apartment. But here's something strange: as they closed the door, one of them, the shorter of the two, took out his handkerchief or a rag and wiped the doorknob and plate. Then when the screen door was closing, he did the same thing to it. Strange, wouldn't you say, Detective, if you were innocent? But if you weren't, you would not want your fingerprints all over the scene, would you? Well, after that, they went down the stairs and walked down the driveway to the alley. When they got past the corner of the garage, I couldn't see them any longer, and I have no idea which way or where they went."

"You didn't see a car?" Gabe asked.

"No. There was no car."

"What time of day was this?"

She responded, "I take my shower between these times every day, come hell or high water, so I am sure of the time frame but not the exact time. However, I would say it was closer to four o'clock, as I remember the afternoon sun appeared waning on the side of the house, but I couldn't swear to that, you understand?"

Olivia Rozane leapt from her chair, reached down to the coffee table to the cigarette box, and retrieved a Camel. She lit it and paced around the room. "You know, Gabe, I wasn't born into this." She gestured with her arms at the room and the house. "I hail from the coalfields of eastern Ohio. My father and old Mark Hannah, that political crook, that dirty old Republican and Ward Healer, were good buddies. When the politics were right, old Mark acquired most of the coalfields in eastern Ohio. He was made the manager of all of it. We had it pretty well for a lot of years, but one day, Dad had to fire one of the miners. He didn't want to, but he had to. The man was a drunk and a wife and child beater who had not been to the mine for over a month. My father called him into his office one morning. He explained all of this to him and told him that he was a drunk and a danger in the mine and that he had no choice but to let him go. The man left my dad's office in an angry state but came back after lunch carrying a 12-gauge double-barrel shotgun. He walked into my father's office and discharged both barrels into him. My father died on the spot. Then this low-life son of a bitch reloaded one barrel and blew his own head off. My father and I were extremely close, and I don't know that I have ever recovered from that tragedy.

"I met George Rozane, another crony of Mark's, at my father's funeral. We started seeing each other, and before I knew it, I was married to him, and we were living in Putnam Landing. The house got built, and I moved in, along with Evelyn Snead. George dropped dead at the plant in 1940, ten years after we were married, and I have been a wealthy widow ever since." She smiled.

Gabe squirmed a bit in his seat. He wasn't one to help another human being. He just wasn't emotionally equipped that way. He lit one of Olivia's Camels and said, "Jeez, I'm sorry about your dad, but, Olivia, do you think you could identify them?"

"Oh, these men? Oh, yes, I could identify the taller of the two, I'm sure."

With that, Gabe rose from the sofa and stuffed out his cigarette, saying, "Well, Olivia, it's so nice to have met you, and I'll return for additional information, if that's all right?"

She looked at him for a few seconds before responding. "Of course, Gabe. Come back any time. I'm here all day, every day, so please, if I can be of further assistance to your cause, come back."

"Thank you, Olivia," he said as he shook her hand. He then found his way out of the sitting room and down the wide stairway. He did not encounter Ms. Snead in the downstairs hall, so he showed himself out of the house.

Gabe noticed Rosary Benedict's car parked across the street as he was going to his car. *What the hell,* he thought as he got into his car and backed out of the driveway. *Where the hell is she?* He thought maybe it was not hers as he drove down the street and headed home. When he arrived home, he called Eloise Fletcher's number, and when she answered, he said, "Hi, Eloise, this is Gabe. How can I help you?"

"What do you mean, how can you help me? You can get over here and see me instead of spending your time on that young twit of a reporter."

"What do you mean, Eloise?" Gabe carefully responded.

"You know exactly what I mean," Eloise firmly stated. "I spent one of the best nights with you that I have had in a long time, and I want more."

Gabe, realizing he had to be very careful, said, "Now, Eloise, our time together was very pleasurable, don't get me wrong, but I am trying to solve a murder case, and I will use anyone who can help me do this. Ms. Benedict and I are professional friends. She is an investigative journalist. I needed to talk with her about some information that she had discovered."

"Yeah, Gabe, and that talk went on until at least four o'clock in the morning. It sure must have been an in-depth talk."

"Oh shit, Eloise, will you stop following me around and spying on me?"

"Damn you, Gabe. You had better visit me this week or else your little chippie at the *Democrat* just might get an interesting story. You know, local detective interviews neighbor and then fucks her. What do you think, Gabe?"

"I'll see you one afternoon next week, Eloise. What about your kids?"

"Not a problem. They're rarely in the house. We don't have to worry."

"Okay, Eloise, see you then," Gabe said as he hung up. *Jesus, this woman has turned into a problem. I wish I would have left her at the Grill instead of bringing her home.* Gabe mixed a drink, lit a cigarette, and reflected on his afternoon at the Rozane house. He also pondered his most recent dilemma, Eloise Fletcher.

That next morning, Atherton and Carl slept in till nine o'clock. They discussed the final plans for the hit on Dr. Marchenko. They planned on being on the water tower by three thirty that afternoon and to wait for him to leave the laboratory. If the car was waiting for him, parked in the usual spot, Carl's shot would be a relatively easy one. He planned on shooting as the rear door was being opened by the officer, in that split second before Marchenko stepped forward to enter the back seat of the car. "One shot, one hit," Carl said. "Then we get out of this place."

"Okay, Carl, that's what I would like to do. We then drive quietly and calmly out of town to Columbus, where we leave the car at the airport and catch a flight back to DC. Now, let's go have breakfast," Thomas said as Carl was opening the motel door to go eat.

The day was overcast and looked as though it might rain. Thomas said, "If it rains, is that going to be a problem for you?"

"I don't think so. I've made kills at longer distances than this in terrible weather conditions."

As they passed through the motel office on their way to the restaurant, Atherton said, "Carl, get a newspaper, and I'll get our table."

Atherton was just sitting down to the table when Carl joined him. "You ain't gonna like this, Thomas." He dropped the morning *Democrat* across Atherton's plate. The headline read, "Wealthy Pottery Widow Can Identify Winston Smith murders."

"Oh shit!" Atherton exclaimed in a whisper.

"Thomas, we've been made by an old lady. What do we do? Do we postpone the hit and take care of her?"

"No," Atherton quietly but emphatically replied. "We carry on. Business as usual, but we must be very careful, nothing out of the ordinary. Do you understand?"

"Yeah, but if that old woman can make us, we may be in trouble."

"I know, Carl. You're right, and that's why we must be very careful."

The two ate their breakfast and returned to the room where Atherton pored over the newspaper.

Gabe St. John was up at six thirty that morning. He went through his usual routine of making coffee and going out to retrieve the morning *Democrat* without looking at it. He tossed the folded newspaper on the kitchen counter next to the coffeepot. He then went to get dressed while the coffee was perking. Upon his return to the kitchen, he poured a cup of the strong java, sat down to the table, and lit a cigarette. As he unfolded the newspaper, he almost choked on his coffee as he read the headlines by Rosary Benedict. "What the fuck!" Gabe stammered as his telephone began ringing off the hook.

The first call was from Chester Matthews, madder than a hornet. "What have you done, St. John? Why didn't you inform the Bureau?"

"Chet, this information just came to me yesterday afternoon, and I haven't talked to anybody, not anybody, especially that Goddamn reporter! I was going to come into the station to make a full report this morning. I have no idea how she got her information."

Agent Matthews made a comment about Gabe having carnal knowledge of the reporter and questioned the possibility of pillow talk.

"Oh, for Christ's sake, you Bible-thumping, fucking moron, do you actually think that I would put the life of a great lady in jeopardy by repeating information to this reporter? Oh, you dumb ass, you had better think again!" Gabe slammed the phone down.

The next time the telephone rang, it was Roy George. "Gabe, what the hell is going on?"

"I don't know. I have no idea. I was coming in to make a full report on this when I read the *Democrat* a few minutes ago. I have not the faintest idea of how Rosary got the story, but I'm going to find out."

Lieutenant George's only comment was, "Get yourself in here. We need to talk."

Gabe called Rosary's apartment, but there was no answer. He hung up the telephone, exclaiming, "Bitch, you are not getting away with this!"

G abe finished his coffee and cigarette and drove to the station where he met with Lieutenant George and related the previous day's events at Olivia Rozane's. George demanded that the detective write a full report before he left the station. "Are you crazy, Roy? That old woman's life is in jeopardy. I have to go see her and tell her that. You'll get your report but not today." Gabe turned and walked out of the lieutenant's office.

He drove to the Rozane house. When he arrived at the large house on Maple Place, he parked under the carport and went to the side door. Evelyn Snead opened the door saying, "Oh, it's you, Detective."

"You're damn right it is, Ms. Snead. I want to see your mistress right now. None of your messing around with house protocol. Now!" Gabe said this as he walked past Ms. Snead at the door.

"Well, uh, Detective, I—"

"You either take me to her or I go and find her. Which is it going to be?"

"I will take you, sir. Please follow me." Ms. Snead's words dripped with sarcastic formality.

Gabe found Olivia Rozane sitting at her large desk writing and smoking. "Detective St. John, hello," she said as she dismissed the housekeeper with a gesture of her hand. "I didn't expect to see you this soon. To what do I owe this visit?"

"Did you read the paper this morning?" Gabe asked her.

"Frankly, no. I do not always read that paper, if you can call it that. In fact, I wouldn't even take it if were called by another name, but *Democrat*, you know, tugs at my heart. Most of the time, it's only good to wrap river carp in. That old stokes who owns it, I swear he's a rotten Republican, and I remember during the war—"

"Olivia!" Gabe interrupted. "We need to talk about an article in this morning's *Democrat*. It's all about you, and I fear that you may be in danger."

Olivia dropped her pen, looking wide-eyed at Gabe. "What the hell do you mean? What kind of danger and from where?"

"Can you get the paper, Olivia?"

With that, Olivia stepped on a button under her credenza, lit a Camel, and the two waited in silence until Ms. Snead appeared in the room. "Evelyn, today's newspaper, where is it?"

Ms. Snead glanced toward Gabe and then back at her mistress and said, "Why, ma'am, it's down in the kitchen."

"I want it. Bring it to me at once," Olivia curtly said to her.

The housekeeper, in an uneasy tone, replied, "Yes, ma'am, I will bring it right away," and she left the room.

"Olivia," Gabe said, breaking the taut silence, "yesterday, as I left your house, I noticed a familiar car parked in front of that big gray house across the street. I believe it belonged to a reporter from the *Democrat*. I believe she was in this house when I left here. She must have been following me yesterday. I'm afraid she got her story from someone in this house because she didn't get any information from me."

"What story, Detective?"

At that moment, the door opened, and Ms. Snead came in with the newspaper. "Here's the newspaper," Ms. Snead remarked as she handed it Olivia and turned to leave the room.

"Just a minute, Evelyn. Was there a reporter here yesterday while Detective St. John was with me?"

"A reporter, ma'am, well, uh, there was a young woman down in the kitchen visiting with Ms. Gillogly for a while," the housekeeper said uneasily.

Olivia lit another cigarette and spoke directly to the housekeeper. "Who in the hell was she and what was she doing in my kitchen, Evelyn?"

"I'm not exactly sure, Mrs. Rozane. She was with Ms. Gillogly."

"And no ands, ifs, or buts, Evelyn, you are the housekeeper, and Goddamn it, I expect you to know who was in my house."

"Well, ma'am, I—"

"No, no, no! You get yourself to the kitchen and bring Mary Katherine up here to me, along with yourself. Do you understand that?"

"Yes, ma'am, I do, and I will be right back."

And with that, a visibly shaken housekeeper left the upstairs sitting room, and Olivia Rozane began reading the paper.

Evelyn Snead descended the long staircase into the large front hall of the house. She walked back under the staircase to a door beside the elevator. Once through that door, she wound her way back to the large kitchen in the back of the house. She could have taken the back stairway directly down to the kitchen, but that was for the common house servants, not for the housekeeper. When she arrived in the kitchen, she found the cook, Mary Katherine Gillogly, a portly woman of Irish Catholic upbringing in her late sixties, busily rolling out a piecrust. She barely acknowledged the housekeeper standing across the table from her. "Mrs. Gillogly, your presence is wanted in the upstairs sitting room."

Mrs. Gillogly, who had been in the household almost as long as Ms. Snead, looked up from her piecrust and exclaimed, "What are you saying, Evelyn? Herself wants me upstairs?"

"That's exactly what I'm saying, Mary Katherine. Now let's go."

"But, but, what's it about? She ain't happy with my cooking after all these years? And me, slaving away in this kitchen from 6:00 a.m. to 7:00 p.m. trying to please them upstairs?"

"No, you're cooking is fine. It's about something else."

"Something else," the cook stated. "I don't know nothing else. I know this kitchen and the meal fixing, and that's it. Now, are you sure that she wants me?" Mrs. Gillogly said as she finished drying her hands.

"Come on, Mary Katherine." And with that, the two women ascended the back stairs, Mrs. Gillogly leading.

Ms. Snead knocked twice, and when she heard Olivia say to come in, Evelyn opened the door, and the two women entered. "I have brought Mrs. Gillogly, as you requested, Mrs. Rozane."

"Good. Please sit down, both of you. Mrs. Gillogly, this is Detective St. John of the Putnam Landing Police Department. Detective, this is my cook and longtime employee, Mrs. Mary Katherine Gillogly."

Before Gabe could acknowledge Mrs. Gillogly, she burst into a half prayer and half lament saying, "Oh, for the love of Mary and all the saints, what have I done, ma'am? A policeman ..." She crossed herself in a state of panic. "Honest, ma'am, I have not been taking anything home from the kitchen. I have not taken or done nothing, ma'am."

"Mary Katherine! Mary Katherine!" Olivia said in a raised voiced. "You have not committed any crime against me or the household. I know that. Detective St. John is not here for you."

"He's not, ma'am? Then why he is here? Has my cookin' gotten that bad? I know them biscuits wasn't quite up to—"

"No, Mrs. Gillogly, no, everything in the kitchen is fine," Olivia reassured her. "The detective is here on another matter, and we just want to ask you some questions."

"Questions, ma'am? What kind of questions? Questions about me husband, Shamus?" Shamus Gillogly would occasionally do yard and other outside work for Olivia when he was sober enough and not sitting in Flood's Bar for the day. "Shamus is a good man, ma'am. Deep down, he's right. He's right with that. He might, he might—"

Olivia pounded her fist on the credenza, yelling, "Mary Katherine Gillogly, will you please be quiet and listen!"

Mrs. Gillogly fell abruptly silent.

Detective St. John, sensing the emotional state of the cook, thought it better to allow Olivia to take the lead in the questioning. "Now, ladies," Olivia went on, "yesterday while I was talking with Detective St. John, was there anyone else in the house, a young woman perhaps?"

The two women looked at each other. Ms. Snead, in a voice cold as ice, responded, "Yes, ma'am. She came to the back door and was in the kitchen talking with Mrs. Gillogly after I came back downstairs. That was after I brought your coffee up, madam."

"Oh, sure, that sweet young thing. A good Catholic girl she is with a name like Rosary. Named after the holy beads, you know. Surely now, Detective, you're not telling me that she's a criminal."

"No, Mrs. Gillogly, she's not a criminal, but what did you two talk about?"

"Well, sir, you see, she was asking questions about them murders next door, she was, and about what I knew about them. I told her the truth, sir, that I knew nothing. I was busy getting the dinner ready, I was. Then Evelyn came into the kitchen, and she began talking to her and telling her about how Mrs. Rozane had seen them two men leaving the house."

The housekeeper squirmed a bit in the chair, looked at the cook with ice-cold eyes, and then said, "Well, yes, madam, I did repeat to her the story that you related to me about seeing the two men on the day of the murder."

The anger showed in Olivia's face and demeanor. She looked at the cook and said, "Mary Katherine, you're excused. You may go back to your duties in the kitchen."

"Yes, ma'am," the cook replied as she stood and left the room.

Ms. Snead rose from her chair and said, "I will get on with my duties as well, madam."

"You, Evelyn, sit down." It was a tone that Evelyn Snead was not accustomed to hearing from the lady of the house, and she complied immediately by dropping back down into her chair.

"Evelyn, I am not just angry with you—I am pissed off!" Olivia said. "You have been the housekeeper of this house since 1932, and you know the responsibilities that your position entails. The main responsibility is that you do not repeat, you do not talk to any outsider about what goes on in this house, nor what is said in this house. My house! Do you understand?"

"Yes, madam, I do, and I am so sorry if I was out of line. It will never happen again. Please, madam, believe me. She was just such a nice young lady and nice to talk with. I just forgot myself. I—"

"Evelyn, that nice young *Catholic* is a reporter from the *Democrat*. She was plying her wiles to obtain information from the two of you, which she embellished for her story, and it was printed in this morning's paper."

The detective said, "And what she wrote very likely could place your mistress in harm's way."

Evelyn Snead looked at Gabe and with a thinly disguised sneer and said, "What you do mean, Detective?"

"Well," Gabe patiently explained, "Ms. Snead, you see, if those two men, those assassins, are still in the area, and we believe that they are, then Olivia here might be in peril."

"How would she be in peril, Detective, from what I said to Ms. Benedict?"

"Consider this, Ms. Snead," Gabe responded. "Two men come into Putnam Landing to commit three murders. They are successful on two of them, but not the third, so they stay in the city or return to it, to finish their job, but in the meantime, they read in the newspaper that there is a witness who can identify them. Being identified is what they don't want. So what might they very well do? Right, kill the witness."

Evelyn Snead sat silently processing the information that Detective St. John had revealed. When she spoke, she did so in a dejected tone, saying, "Detective, I am an old woman. I came to this house as a young girl, and I have grown old with its walls. I have not ventured outside, and I know very little about the world. This house has been my world. So when a fresh young woman arrives here, I talk too much, not knowing, you understand, that I am talking too much about the operation of this house and my responsibilities to it and to Mrs. Rozane. I am heartedly sorry if anything that I have divulged has placed Mrs. Rozane or anyone else in jeopardy. I don't know what else to say." Sensing Ms. Snead's deep sense of mea culpa, the detective fell silent.

Olivia too was at a loss for words. She only said, "Very well, Evelyn. Please carry on with your duties." Ms. Snead rose and left the room. Detective St. John saw tears welling up in her stoic eyes as she exited.

"Oh well, shit, Gabe. I suppose to a large extent I'm to blame for Evelyn. I never encouraged her to have a life outside of this house. This house has been, is, her life. She's as sheltered and naïve as the virgin who's been locked in the closet by her father. Don't concern yourself about me. I have this." Olivia pulled out of her desk drawer a Browning 9 mm automatic. "George brought this home to me on one of his trips to England. He and I shot it until I could hit a bull's-eye at twenty yards, and believe me, I still can. It has worked for the Brits, and it works for me."

"Well, Olivia, okay. Keep it handy as you may need it, but please don't hesitate to call me anytime," Gabe said.

"I won't, and thank you for your concern."

With that, the detective stood up, bade goodbye to Olivia, and retraced his way out of the house. It was still a cloudy day. *Damn,* he thought, *I need a sunny day.* It was well after noon, and Gabe was hungry, so he thought, *I'll swing by Kate's on my way to the station for a quick sandwich.*

therton and Waters had been held up in their room since breakfast. They had been going over their plans and discussing the next-door neighbor who could identify them as leaving Diane Smith's apartment on the day of the hit. Thomas was not too concerned about Olivia Rozane, stating to Carl, "She's an old woman who saw two figures. I don't believe she can identify us from that distance. Besides, there's no time to do anything about her. We have to take out the scientist and get out of town."

Carl felt otherwise. "She's a threat to us and to the organization we work for. I'm in favor of removing that threat."

"Well, how do you propose we do that, Carl? Do we take the shot at Marchenko and then nonchalantly swing by that neighborhood on our way out of town and shoot the old lady—that is, with every cop in the county swarming all over the city and beyond, plus a houseful of servants in the woman's house? Do we just shoot all of them as well? No, Carl! We hit Marchenko and get the hell out of town. Hopefully ahead of the police."

"But we're leaving a witness, and you know what the colonel says. We don't leave witnesses."

"Screw him! We're not mass murderers, Carl. I am still not understanding this whole Marchenko thing. It still doesn't add up. Why are we taking out a top-level scientist who has proven his worth to this country by developing a guidance system that can drop a missile into Khrushchev's lap while he's eating breakfast? And why is Colonel Corbin so hell-bent on the job being done yesterday?"

Carl wryly replied, "We're just mechanics, Tommy boy, just mechanics."

Atherton pondered Carl's words before replying, "Yep, we go where they send us. We kill whomever they tell us. We don't question. We keep our mouth shut. We get paid. We wait for the next job. Well, Carl, I'm thinking this just might be my last job as a mechanic."

"You mean you're getting out? You're leaving the company? Can you just do that?"

"I don't see why not."

"You know too much, Thomas. You know where too many skeletons are buried. They'll never let you leave alive."

"There are ways, Carl. There are ways," Atherton replied.

Detective St. John had spent a mundane afternoon at his office. Kate's lunch had turned into a three-course meal, and by one thirty, Gabe found himself nodding off at his desk. He had been trying to reach Agent Matthews but to no avail. He had talked to Sylvia and listened to her raving about the damned attorneys in regard to Zane's estate and the fact that Gabe had not been to see her. He had even tried to reach Eloise Fletcher, remembering the lovely patch of auburn hair between her thighs. He thought that he might stop at her house for a brief encounter. She too did not answer her phone, so at a quarter to two, he decided to head home for a lie down and then go from there. He left the station. The day was still cloudy with periods of bright, broken sun.

When he arrived home, a man was sitting on his porch steps. Gabe was poised to retrieve his .38 from under his left armpit when the man said, "You old son of a bitch, it's been years." Gabe was taken aback. It was then that he recognized the man—Leo Winthrop, Gabe's good friend from high school. He had seen him only one time since their graduation.

Leo had left Putnam Landing and gone to Athens to attend Ohio University. Upon graduating from Ohio University, he went to Illinois, where he earned both a master's degree and a doctorate in history from some college in Chicago. Gabe never knew the name of it, only that it was in Chicago. As they shook hands and entered the house, both men had years of catching up to do. Gabe mixed drinks, and the two men settled in for a long, drunken visit.

Gabe looked at Leo, who had not changed any except for a full beard, and said, "I haven't seen you since your father died right after the war. What's been happening with you since you left town? We really didn't visit at your father's funeral, other than you telling me you were finished with school and you were working and living in Chicago."

"Well, Gabe, that's about all there is to tell you. I was finishing the bachelor's degree at OU, the war clouds were looming. I made it to Chicago and started graduate studies. The Japs hit Pearl Harbor that December, and I thought for sure I would be drafted, but no, nothing, so I kept on studying and working until I earned the master's degree. Then the History Department at St. Edward the Confessor offered me the opportunity to earn a doctorate. Gabe, I honestly felt guilty that I wasn't in uniform, but I thought that once I finished, I would be more valuable to the war effort with the advanced degree. So I accepted their offer and began working on the doctorate. In 1943, I knew they were going to draft me, so I interrupted my studies and joined the navy."

"Well, were you on a ship? Did you see action in the Pacific?" Gabe asked as he lit a cigarette and refilled their drinks.

"No and no," Leo responded. "When they saw what I had been doing, they put me into Naval Intelligence and stationed me right there in Chicago. I couldn't believe my luck. I worked for the navy during the day and attended classes at St. Edwards at night. Then in June of '44, they sent me to England. My professor signed off on my course work and told me to start writing a dissertation. I guess good ole St. Edwards did its part for the war effort, as by the time my ship landed in England, I had a good start on my writing.

"In England, the training was pretty intense, as I was with Special Operations Executive, the SOE. They put us on a dilapidated Swedish fishing boat and set us on course for the coast of Germany. Well, actually, the island of Peenemünde just off the north German coast in the Baltic Sea. You know, where the V-2s were being launched. We sat on that damn scow for the duration, receiving all types of information from photographs to radio intercepts. You name it. We floated there, relating that stuff back to London and dodging German patrol boats. Gabe, I have a box full of that stuff out on your porch that I would like you to see. Well, Peenemünde was finally taken by the Allies. We were picked up by a Royal Navy destroyer. Our pathetic boat was sunk, and I was able to complete the doctorate, and here I am back in Putnam Landing, ready to start a new job and look for a place to live."

"Wow," Gabe exclaimed to his friend, "it seems as though you've had a hell of a war, Leo."

"I must say, I really can't figure out why one of those Kraut patrol boats didn't sink us. They didn't even board us. They would pull up alongside, look us over, give us a wave, and sail on. If they would have come aboard, they would have shot all of us and sent the scow to the bottom of the North Sea."

Gabe rose and went to the kitchen to refill their drinks. While he did this, Leo went to the front porch to bring in the rest of his gear, including the box of photos and files. Gabe returned to the living room as Leo was coming through the door with his belongings. Gabe dropped to the couch, lit a cigarette, and said, "What do you need, Leo?"

Leo took a sip of his drink and sat down. "I have a job here in Putnam Landing teaching history at the Ohio University branch. I'm going to need a place to live, and I was hoping I could stay with you until I found an apartment."

"Sure," Gabe responded. "Stay as long as you need to."

Leo began to pull photographs from his box and spread them on the coffee table in front of Gabe. "These pictures are fascinating. They're from inside the Peenemünde facility. They came from a Pole who was part of the Nazis' forced laborers but who was working for us. He was invaluable to us. He somehow was able to take these pictures and smuggle them out to us."

"But, Leo, you shouldn't have these, should you? I mean, wouldn't the government shoot you or something if they knew you had them?"

"Or something is right, Gabe. I did most of the film development, and for those that I found interesting, I made copies for me. That is what these are. Many of those goose-stepping Nazi sons of bitches are now living the high life and enjoying the fruits of democracy right here in the good old US of A."

Gabe stubbed out his cigarette and said, "Are you kidding me?"

"No, sir. Among the various intelligence agencies, the Allied governments, and the OSS, there were well over a hundred ex-Nazis who were given clean papers and passports and sent to the States. And those were only the ones I worked on between London and Marseilles. Think of the rest of Europe and how many more there could be. They were all scientists, engineers, mathematicians, physicists, chemists, people like that. I'm telling you, our government didn't care who they were or what atrocities they had been part of. They packed them up and brought them here to work on our missile and atomic programming."

Gabe thought for minute. "Wait a minute. Wait just a Goddamn minute! Did you ever hear of a Russian physicist named Marchenko? Dr. Victor Marchenko? He worked for the Germans at Peenemünde until the Allies got there. He then arrived in the US at Putnam Landing, Ohio."

"Victor Marchenko? Oh, hell yes, I know that name. He worked with the Polish laborer getting us pictures and information. In fact, we gave him the code name Camel because he went the duration without being caught or even aided in any way. He was invaluable to the Allies and the war effort, and you're telling me that he's right here in Putnam Landing?"

"Yep, he sure is. Right here at Winston Optics."

"I'll be damned, Gabe. I want to meet him."

"You want to meet him? I thought you knew him."

"Well, not really," Leo replied. "I only knew him from his radio messages and from the film he smuggled out to us. Even at war's end, I never actually met up with him, but his paperwork and documents were some of the first ones that I remember working on." As Leo was talking, Gabe was perusing the twenty or so pictures spread out on the coffee table.

Suddenly, Gabe said, "Oh my gosh, Leo, there he is! He's a little younger, but it's for sure Dr. Marchenko." Gabe rose and took the photograph to Leo to identify Marchenko. "That's him, right there," he said, pointing to Victor sitting around a large conference table, accompanied by nine or ten German officers of various ranks. "Who are these guys with Marchenko?" Gabe questioned.

"Those are the officers and the scientists at Peenemünde. We know them all now, except for this guy sitting right here in civilian dress," Leo said as he pointed to the man in the business suit sitting at the table, "and we could never find him or anyone who has been able to identify him. The radio intel that we got from Camel, Marchenko, did not identify him. The only thing it said was something to the order of he attended a two-day conference and never spoke, kept to himself at all times. He's still our mystery man."

The mystery man at the table was a large man with white hair who was smoking a cigarette—not that this was unusual, as several others were smoking as well, but Gabe looked more closely at the pack of cigarettes lying in front of him. He was sure they were Camels. "American cigarettes," Gabe commented.

"What that, Gabe?"

"Well, I can't tell for sure, but that pack of cigarettes sure looks like Camels."

"Camels. Let me see that," Leo said as he reached for the photograph. "Damn, I think you're right, Gabe. Those are Camels. On second thought though, that's not too unusual, as the Krauts loved our cigarettes. They were usually the first taken from a dead GI or a POW."

"Yeah," Gabe said, "I do remember that."

Leo stood up, saying, "I need the john. Where is it?"

Gabe told him the way to the bathroom, and as Leo walked out of the living room, Gabe placed the photograph into his shirt pocket. He wasn't sure why he had done that. He just did.

Leo returned to the living room to a fresh drink. As he sat down, he looked a Gabe and said, "What the hell is going on in this sleepy little hamlet? Murder! Murders! Zane Winston of all people, a shootout at Holy Rosary? What's going on?"

For the next hour, Gabe tried to explain to Leo what was happening in Putnam Landing, omitting some information, such as the radio and guns and the fact that Diane Smith was a Soviet agent.

At 5:20, Gabe's phone rang. It was Betty from the station. "Gabe, there's been a shooting at Winston Optics, an attempt to kill Dr. Marchenko. One of his officers and his chauffer are down!"

"Christ, Betty! I'll be right there."

Atherton and Carl had spent the day in their motel room with Thomas cautiously looking through the window from time to time to view the parking lot. "I thought everything was okay, Tommy boy. Are you thinking that old lady might be sitting out there waiting to pop us when we step out the door?" Carl said as he mixed another bourbon.

"Carl, you're drinking too heavily for the job we have to do. You're placing us in jeopardy."

"Tommy, my boy, don't you worry about a thing. Old Carl is steady as a rock. Well, I remember once during the war, I had to kill a Kraut major. Well, I tell you, I had been drinking wine all day. Damn, I'll tell you, those Frogs can make a bottle of wine. Well, here I am, ready—"

"Carl, Goddamn it! You aren't in France shooting Germans any longer. You, we, goddamn it, have a job to do. It is a precision job, and nothing can go wrong, and if it does and we have to chase that old Russian back to his lair, we are fucked! Do you understand that, Carl? We are more than likely dead man."

"Thomas, I'm fine. I'll take the shot and make it. Even the weather is cooperating. A nice overcast day."

The two left the motel at three o'clock. Thomas went to the office to pay their bill and check out. As he tried to leave, the desk girl said, "Thank you, sir. Please come back." Atherton gestured a wave with his hand and never looked around at her. They left the parking lot and headed for the old water tower on top of the Dillon woods. As they drove through Putnam Landing, it became obvious to Atherton that Carl was not at his best. He was rambling loudly one minute, and then the next, he would momentarily doze off. "Carl, will you fucking wake up and get ahold of yourself?" The sun was poking out from the clouds for a few minutes at a time.

Atherton parked the car on the heavily rutted road, and they disembarked with Carl carrying the disassembled M1 sniper rifle in a soft cloth bag. They ascended the small hill up to its crest, then descended a few feet down on the other side to the water tower. Once on the catwalk, Carl assembled the M1, put the silencer on the end of the barrel, and began sighting in the parking lot just below. The two assassins then sat and waited for Dr. Marchenko to appear. While they waited, Atherton made up his mind to get out—enough of this killing, especially without ever being told why. The colonel just handing him a large envelope and saying, "Here is your next assignment," with no talk or explanation other than kill. He had done it, and he had been the good soldier for God and the American way, but no more, especially after this one. Why this one? It just didn't square with Atherton. He had a sizable bank account, and he and Cheryl could live comfortably the rest of their lives somewhere in South America. As soon as this job was finished, he would disappear with Cheryl.

"Well, Tommy boy, get ready," Carl's voice had shaken Atherton out of his planning. "His car is just pulling into the parking lot."

Atherton shook off his daydreaming and became alert. It was a quarter to five and close to time for action. Carl was busy adjusting the telescope of the M1 to get it just right. The door of the plant opened, and Marchenko began walking across the parking lot to his car. Carl followed him in the telescope. When he arrived at his car, one of the officers assigned to him opened the left rear door for Victor. Carl had a beautiful shot and began to gently apply pressure on the M1's trigger. As he was executing his shot, the sun broke through the clouds, and a bright ray of light hit the windshield of the Cadillac, causing a glare and a reflection back through the telescope of the M1, temporarily blinding

Carl. The rifle went off, and Carl yelled, "Damn!" The shot shattered the rear window, missing Marchenko. The officer pushed Victor into the car, ordering him to lie on the floor as he drew his service revolver and crouched behind the open rear door. He was trying to determine where the shot originated, but due to the silencer on the rifle, it was difficult. The other officer, who was behind the car, began randomly shooting at the hill. The cop behind the door scanned the hill and spotting the water tower thought that was the logical place for a shooter to be. Just then, the driver of the Cadillac got out of the car with his pistol drawn. A second shot struck him below his left eye. He fell dead in the parking lot. The officer behind the door raised his .38, aiming for just about the top of the old water tower and squeezed off two rounds. Both hit just above the assassins. Water began to pour out from where the bullets struck.

"Damn!" Carl exclaimed. "That guy's good." Just then, two more shots were fired. One barely missed Atherton, and the other struck Carl just below the right shoulder. "Oh shit!" he screamed as he fell back against the tower. "He got me. That lucky son of a bitch got me with a handgun."

Atherton looked to his left and saw a growing spot of red spreading across Carl's right breast. "Oh damn! What a freak shot! That motherfucker is very good or very lucky," Carl angrily said as he struggled to pick up the rifle for one more shot.

"What the hell are you doing, Carl? We've got to get out of here!"

"Not before I get that motherfucker!" Carl murmured as he struggled to strike the rifle. He drew a bead on the open door and squeezed the trigger. The shot pierced the door and penetrated the officer in his left chest. He fell over dead. "Okay, Tommy, let's get out of here."

When they got into the car, Thomas said, "Hold on, Carl. We'll get out of here." But by the time he reached Linden Avenue, Carl was dead. He had bled out. Atherton sat at the intersection trying to think how to handle Carl's body. The parking lot at Winston Optics was ablaze with police and emergency vehicles.

It was then that he remembered the boat dock road about a quarter mile north of where he sat. He eased the car, turning to the left, trying not to call attention to himself. They had found the access road, which was just north of Victor Marchenko's house on the hill, when they were searching for the door to the tunnel. The road was no more than two tire tracks, which led to the river and appeared to be used to launch boats for fishing and for pleasure. There were no houses near it and no people there. Atherton thought it might be a good spot to dispose of Carl's body, so he headed down the access road toward the river. He drove down to the wide spot where the road met the Elk Eye and was used as a turnabout to launch the boats.

Thomas drove to the water's edge and parked the car parallel to the Elk Eye, being mindful not to get mired in the river mud and water. He dragged the body out of the car and waded about ten yards into the river. The water was up to his belt, and he sensed that going out any farther would result in a drop-off, so he let go of the body and watched it float in the current downstream and then gently sink into the depths of the river. The M1 was next. Atherton took it by the end of the barrel and slung it out into the water. He then returned to the car, soaking wet and uncomfortable. He wondered, *What now? How can I salvage this fucked-up situation?* His thoughts momentarily wandered to Cheryl with her soft, full lips and body, her absolute loyalty to him, her love for him. But first, he had a job to complete. Marchenko had to be killed. He was an enemy of the state who had to be eliminated. Yet, was he? Atherton shook his head as if to erase all doubts and proceeded up the hill to Marchenko's house.

21

Detective St. John hung up the phone and went to the living room closet where his pistols were hanging in their holsters. He quickly opted for the .38 Super. While wiggling into the soft leather holster, he told Leo to make himself at home. "I have to go, Leo. There's been a shooting." Gabe was putting on his sports coat as he walked.

Leo yelled, "Be careful!" as Gabe stepped out onto the front porch.

Pulling into the parking lot of Winston Optics, he was greeted by every cop in Putnam Landing, including Lieutenant George and the chief. Three ambulances were there, as well as several deputy sheriffs. It was chaos. As soon as he stepped out of his car, he was accosted by none other than Rosary Benedict from the *Democrat*. "Gabe, what happened? No one will talk to me. Who got shot? What's going on?"

"I don't know anything. I'm just getting here myself. Give me some time."

"Damn, you Gabe! There is no time. I want information about this, and I want it now." Rose began closing in on Gabe, along with her cameraman, who was snapping pictures.

Gabe motioned for the nearest uniform, saying, "Move these two now!"

The officer gently but firmly pushed the reporters back behind the police lines, with Rosary yelling at Gabe as she moved. "You bastard!

You owe me! You owe me!" Her voice trailed off, mingling with the many others that were at the scene.

Gabe walked to Lieutenant George. "What happened, Roy?"

"Not too sure, Gabe, other than someone tried to murder Dr. Marchenko." Lieutenant George appeared to be out of his element.

Christ, Gabe thought, *he looks confused*. "Do we have the shooter?"

"No," Lieutenant George replied, "we don't."

"Where did it happen? Was the shooter in the parking lot?"

"I don't know. But we think the shots might have come from up there," Lieutenant George said as he pointed to the wooded hill and water tower.

"Has that area been searched?"

"Not yet, Gabe. We've been too busy here."

"Too busy, Roy?" He let it drop and called a patrolman. "Bernie."

"Yes, sir," the officer responded.

"Take three or four of these guys and check out that hillside." Gabe gestured with a nod to the hill. "And pay close attention to that old water tower of the Putnam Landing Tile."

"Yes, sir, Detective, we're on our way." The young officer began selecting four other uniforms to help him in the search.

Out of the corner of his eye, Gabe caught sight of Dr. Eli by one of the ambulances. He walked over to him. "What do we have, Doc?"

"We have a professional shooter picking off people from a long distance with a high-powered rifle, and we cannot even be sure where the shots came from."

"Wouldn't a report from the rifle give an indication of where they came from?"

"Yes, Gabe, they would, they would have, but there was no sound. Nothing. I'm sure that the rifle had a silencer on it."

"Jesus, Eli, do you really think that?"

"Absolutely. The rounds that hit these men were devastating. I'm sure they were dead before they ever hit the ground. A rifle that powerful would have been heard all over this end of town, but nobody heard anything. We have talked to people in this crowd—and nothing. They heard nothing."

Gabe lit a cigarette, and while he surveyed the chaos of the scene, the radio in his car began squawking. He moved to answer it, discovering that the voice was that of Bernie Murphy, the officer he had sent to check out the hill. "Detective," the voice crackled, "this is Officer Murphy."

"Yes, Bernie, what did you find?"

"Sir, I think you had better come up here and see for yourself."

"Bernie, what is it?"

"Sir, we have found three empty casings and blood. Blood everywhere, sir, on the tower, on the ground, a trail leading—"

"I'll be right there, Bernie. Tell me how to get to you."

"Well, sir, come up Taylor Street and turn onto Oakwood. Follow Oakwood to the end and then turn right. There's a heavily rutted access road through the fields back to where we are behind the water tower. I'll meet you there."

"Okay, Bernie, I'm on my way." Gabe stepped on his cigarette and went to Lieutenant George. "Roy, the guys up on the hill found something. I'm going up there now."

"What? What guys on the hill?"

"The ones I sent up there. I'll be back." Gabe got into this car and headed for the water tower.

Gabe carefully negotiated the deep ruts in the contractors' access road back to the water tower. Once there, Office Murphy and the other patrolman met him. "Sir, look at this." Murphy was pointing to a blood trail leading up to the woods.

"That appears to be a significant wound with a lot of blood loss."

"Yes, sir, it does, and this is where it ends. The car must have been parked right here. The trail leads back to the water tank where there's a lot more blood."

"Good job, Bernie. Let's go look." They approached the water tower, and the blood trail was more pronounced. When Gabe climbed the tower to the catwalk, the amount of blood intensified.

"Sir, could this person have survived this wound?"

"I'm not too sure, Bernie, but let's get an expert opinion." Gabe motioned to one of the officers, telling him to return to his patrol car and radio down to the crime scene for the coroner and request that he come up there. The young officer did as requested, and in about ten minutes, Dr. Eli was on the scene.

"No, Gabe, a man losing this much blood could not survive."

"You mean we have a dead assassin somewhere?"

"Gabe, a person losing this much blood must have a severed artery. There's no way he could have made it. Not even with immediate medical treatment."

Officer Murphy showed Gabe the empty shell casings that were found on the water tower and on the ground below. Gabe examined the three casings, commenting, "There are no markings, no caliber, no manufacture, no nothing."

Eli looked at them and said, "Wow, Gabe, you have quite a job facing you. I would guess these are a 30.06 or a .308, but who knows for sure. I don't understand how there are no markings."

"Me neither, Doc. Maybe the lab can tell us something."

With that, they left the water tower and returned to Winston Optics parking lot.

22

Thomas Atherton drove up the hill leading to Victor Marchenko's house. The house sat a hundred yards from the road with a large fence surrounding it. With the summer vegetation and trees, it was difficult to see the house. As he approached the drive, there were two shotgun-wielding police officers manning the gate. Thomas drove by knowing that if there were two visible cops, there would be at least five more on the grounds and in the house. He also knew as he drove up the hill that there was no place to park a car or to pull off the road. He and Carl had checked that out quite thoroughly during their week in Putnam Landing when they were trying to formulate a plan B in the event that plan A failed, as it had. They had come to the conclusion that with just the two of them, experienced though they were, there was no backup plan. They would have been apprehended or killed trying to get to the house. "Small-town cops work that way," Atherton had told Carl, "Overkill is their mantra." Carl looked puzzled, and Thomas had explained. *Mantra.* Atherton smiled briefly, remembering their conversation. He then turned around in a driveway, waving to the homeowner who was mowing his lawn. As he was preceding back down the hill, it hit him. "The tunnel, that Goddamn tunnel. That's the way into the house," he said as he passed the cops at the gate once again. "By God, I'm going to get a shot at Marchenko. They may get me, but I will get him." He reached Linden Avenue. Straight across the street at the railroad tracks was a small marina and boat repair operation of the old captain's.

It was eight o'clock on this June evening as Atherton slowly drove across Linden Avenue into the marina. He crossed the railroad tracks and idled down the narrow drive to the boat docks on the Elk Eye. He backed his car slightly down into one of the concrete boat launches so that he could drive out faster, should he be so lucky. He figured that he could spend the time between dusk and dark by sitting on the pier watching the river flow by. At dark, he would go to the spot on the bank where he was pretty sure the door was. Atherton had located it when he and Carl were poking around on the bank. He had said nothing to Carl. Sometimes with Carl, the least said, the better. As Atherton stood outside the car, he noticed that the large boat that had been tied up to the dock was gone. He and Carl had both commented on its beauty and lines.

As Atherton stood looking at the empty pier, a voice came from out of the dusk. "Yep, she's gone. She's a beauty, ain't she?" Atherton turned around to find a short, muscular, barrel-chested man in his middle years, standing on the cement wall of the boat launch, lighting his pipe. "We've got two of them," he went on to say, "so if you want her sister, she's in the boat shed undergoing some work. She'll be seaworthy in two days and available for rent."

"For rent? What are you talking about?"

"I thought you might have been looking to rent one."

"Oh, no, I just admired it," Atherton said as he approached the pipe-smoking man.

"We have two of them you know, both Chris-Crafts. Best boats made. You know, we rent them out for weekends and holidays during the season."

"Oh yes, of course," Atherton responded, "but what about the one that was here? Where is it?"

"I'm not sure, sir. It's leased for the entire year by some foreign fellow. I couldn't tell you where it is, but it left about a half hour ago heading south. If you want her sister, she will be ready in two days."

"No, I don't. I just love the water and beautiful boats, especially at night."

The man had a noticeable tick. Every few minutes, his head would twitch. He continued puffing on his pipe and stated, "This twitch is from Korea. The captain and I, we went through the Pacific killing Japs and then through Korea killing Koreans and Chinks, and this is left over from Korea. They don't know why, but I got it. The captain hired me, and we're still together. I just live right there in that cottage." He pointed to the small house on the riverbank as he tapped out the cottle from his pipe. "You have a good evening." With that, he walked back to his house.

Atherton walked to the steep bank where it was thick with scrub bushes and other weeds. He was just about to begin poking and feeling when he discovered a large hole, an opening in the bank. There it was. The door of the tunnel, wide open. Stunned, he was processing this when it hit him. The Chris-Craft being leased to a foreigner, the tunnel door kicked open, the boat gone for thirty minutes. "Shit! He's gone."

23

I t was nearly ten o'clock when an exhausted Gabe finally made it home. All he wanted was a long, hot shower and sleep. He quietly entered the house so as not to bother Leo, but Leo was nowhere to be seen. Gabe found a note from him saying, "Quite tired from the driving, our visit, and the alcohol. I will see you in the morning. Hope all went well. Thanks for the bed. P. S. Two numbers that you need to call." Gabe recognized one number as being Sylvia's. The second one was the station. He called the station first. Detective McGee answered the phone.

"Frank, this is Gabe. I'm returning a call from about an hour ago."

"Oh, yeah, Gabe. You're needed at the Marchenko house right away. That old scientist has disappeared."

"Disappeared! What the fuck! How did that happen?"

"He's gone. Somehow he eluded the blues in the house and is gone."

"Why the hell didn't you call me on the radio, Frank?"

"Gabe, you know me. I never could use that thing from this end, and Betty is gone."

"Oh, shit, Frank!" Gabe slammed down the receiver. He put his shoulder holster and sports jacket back on and ran out the door.

Two policemen had accompanied Victor Marchenko into his house about seven thirty. One went room to room with revolver drawn, putting on lights and checking for intruders. The second remained with Victor in the spacious living room of the house. Victor, somewhat shaken from his close call with death, went to the bar at the end of the room. He poured a glass of Hennessey and soda, walked to the couch, and sat down. The officer with him asked if he was okay and offered him a cigarette. "Yes, yes, I will be fine, and no thank you. I shall have one of these." Victor opened the humidor on the coffee table and took out a punch cigar. He trimmed the end off it and lit it. "I will be fine, Officer, in a while. Just allow me to savor my cigar and brandy. Help yourself, if you wish."

"No thank you, sir. I'm fine."

The first officer returned to the living room with an all clear as Victor sat imbibing and enjoying the cigar. The wheels were turning in his head. He knew that he was not safe. These policemen could not protect him. He knew that he must get down the basement and to the tunnel, out to the boat that he had rented for the year and make his escape. Victor smoked half the cigar and then laid it in the large ashtray. He finished the brandy and soda and then explained, "Gentleman, I must use the bathroom."

Both policemen came to attention, one saying, "Earl, go with him."

"Oh, please, no," Marchenko said. "I must have some privacy. The bathroom is just down the hall. Please, Officers."

The two cops looked at each other. One said, "Okay, Doc, go and come right back."

"Thank you both." Marchenko left for the bathroom. He walked past the bathroom straight into the kitchen to the basement door. Entering the basement stairway, he retrieved the key to the Chris-Craft hanging on the peg. He proceeded to open the door to the tunnel, turned on the light switch, picked up a flashlight, and went down the dimly lit steps to the river.

Gabe arrived at the Marchenko house at 10:20. He immediately asked, "What the hell happened?"

"Well, sir," one of the uniforms began, "we got into the house, checked it out, found nothing. Marchenko fixed a drink, lit a cigar, and sat down right there." The officer pointed to the sofa. "He sat here and finished his drink and most of the cigar. Then he asked to go to the bathroom, so we let him go. He left the room, and we never saw him again. We waited for about ten minutes and went to check on him. He was nowhere to be found. We checked the downstairs to the house and the basement—and nothing. He just vanished."

"Horseshit, you two! You," Gabe said, gesturing at the closest officer, "come with me." The two went through the hall, stopping at the restroom and looking into it. Gabe moved into the kitchen. Checking the back door and finding it locked from the inside, he moved to a door across the kitchen. Once he opened it, he discerned it was the basement. The lights were still on, so Gabe and the patrolman descended the stairs. "Do you have your flashlight, Officer?" Gabe asked as they were going down.

"Yes, sir, I do."

"Good, we may need it." The large basement was well lighted expect for one room in the back. The detective and patrolman shown the light and carefully examined the room. There appeared to be nothing there, but Gabe said, "Let's look more closely." With that, the two men began to shine the light carefully on the walls as they moved along them. When they got to a back corner, Gabe noticed a small latch protruding from the wall. "What's this?" he wondered as he lifted the latch and pulled on it. As he did this, the door swung open to reveal a lighted set of steps. "Whoa, what is this and where does it go?"

"Damn if I know, sir. Are we going down there?"

"You bet. Come on." They proceeded down the steps as Gabe marveled at the architecture. "My God, these are poured concrete steps—and look at the vaulted concrete walls and ceiling."

The officer made no comment other than, "Uh huh."

At the end of the steps, the tunnel widened, and both men could walk upright. They turned on the flashlight as the electric lights were failing. "Jesus, who built this and why?" was Gabe's only comment as they at last approached the exit. The last fifteen to twenty feet, they both had to crawl until they exited under the railroad track at the marina. "For Christ's sake, this is where Marchenko went, but where did he go from here?" Gabe said.

"Hell, I don't know, Detective. This is spooky. Who would build something like this anyway, and why would they build it?"

"I don't know, but we're going to find out." They dusted themselves off, and Gabe noticed a light on in a small house on the riverbank. "Come on, we're gonna go ask some questions but say nothing about this tunnel. You understand?"

"I do, Detective, and I'll say nothing."

They proceeded to the cottage and knocked on the door. A man responded to the knock, asking, "Yes, what do you want?"

Gabe flashed his badge, saying, "Sir, we need information."

The man with the twitch related his earlier observation of the Chris-Craft leaving the dock and his conversation with the stranger by the river. He explained again about the Chris-Crafts and the one that was rented for the year to some old fellow with an accent. "I think he lives somewhere around here."

Gabe didn't respond to that but asked, "He went south?"

"That's right," the man said, pointing in the direction that the boat went.

"But the dam," Gabe stated.

"Yes, sir, but there's a canal, you know?"

"Oh shit, the canal. Can that get under the bridge or does your span have to be lifted?"

"You know, I honestly don't remember if the Chris-Crafts will clear that span or not. They are fine boats, you know, and these are two of the finest. They have about a twenty-foot super structure, but I don't remember if they'll clear without the span being raised. Normally, we could give the captain a call, but he left for vacation yesterday, and I don't remember," he said with a tick.

"It's okay, but are you sure he went south?" Gabe asked.

"Positive. Yes, sir. I watched it go down the river."

"Thank you for your time, sir. We will be leaving you now."

"Come back anytime, boys. I'm always here."

"We have to get down to the dam," he said as they arrived in the parking lot. Then it hit him. "Shit, we don't have a car." Gabe surveyed the parking lot, looking for a vehicle. The only thing drivable was a Ford tractor parked behind the cottage that they had just left. He ran over to it, searching for the key, thinking there was no way the key would be there, but it was in the ignition switch. He climbed up in the seat and turned the key. The engine came alive with a loud rumble. "I'm not sure I can drive this thing but ..."

"Sir! Detective!" the young officer yelled above the din of the motor. "I was raised on a farm just out the pike. I can drive it."

Gabe jumped out of his perch and helped pull the officer up to the driver's seat. "Get us up the hill to the car—quick!"

"Yes, sir, but you hold on."

Gabe did just that, and in a matter of moments, the young patrolman had them up onto Linden Avenue and approaching Hilltop Lane.

The two uniforms aimed the shotguns at the tractor and the two figures aboard. Gabe began yelling, "No, no, hold your fire! It's Detective St. John and Officer Murphy. Don't shoot!"

The two officers lowered their weapons and opened the gate. "You two going to plow the back forty, Detective?"

Gabe directed Officer Murphy to the house where the car was parked, and as he turned off the tractor's engine, the front door opened. It was the other officer of the house detail. "Earl!" Gabe yelled. "Get another officer and meet us at the lift span on the canal." Earl looked confused, and Gabe said, "Now! The lift span on the canal. Let's go!" Gabe was running to his car with young Murphy in tow. They jumped into the car and sped off for the canal.

Marchenko had exited the tunnel and dashed across the open space to where the Chris-Craft was docked. He set about freeing her landlines and jumped aboard, climbing up to the bridge where he turned the key, bringing the powerful six-cylinder engine to life. He carefully maneuvered her away from the dock and out into the channel. The Chris-Craft prodded slowly down the Elk Eye toward the dam. Marchenko knew that it might be difficult to find the entrance into the canal at night, but he pressed on, moving the big boat slowly along until he was up on it. He carefully steered the boat into the mouth of the canal with no problems. As he approached the lift span, he sped up, the large engine churning up the water as he proceeded under the span. Then the sound that no boater ever wants to hear happened. There was a loud crashing of wood being smashed, accompanied by the awful sound of bending and snapping steel. The boat was stuck under the lift span of the bridge. The super structure came down around Marchenko with some of it falling on him. His head was struck, and he was stunned and bleeding.

Atherton was watching all of this from the canal bank, and the moment the boat struck the bridge, he was in the water, heading for Marchenko. He had taken off his sports jacket and shoes and was holding the .38 high out of the water as he swam to the boat's ladder. Atherton knew that he had to work quickly, as the noise from the accident might alert people and cause a commotion. He adroitly climbed the ladder and worked his way to what was left of the bridge. There he located Victor sitting among the rubble and still in a daze. Atherton leveled the pistol at Marchenko's head. *One shot*, he thought. *Then I'm out of here.* He pulled the hammer back to cock the pistol for firing, but at that moment, a bright light flashed in among the rubble, catching him in its beam. A voice from the canal bank yelled, "Is anybody hurt? There's an ambulance on the way. We'll be over to you in just a minute."

Looking at the bank, Atherton saw two policemen shining their squad car spotlight into the wreckage. It looked also as if there were figures in the water approaching the boat. He was trying to pull Marchenko up from the floor to use him as a shield to help him escape. By the time he had accomplished that, Detective St. John and Officer Murphy had boarded the Chris-Craft and were heading for the wheelhouse. Atherton aimed and fired one shot, missing Gabe but striking young Murphy in the neck. He died in agony as he choked on his own blood.

Gabe was trying to clear his head as Atherton yelled, "I've got the old man and will put a bullet through his brain if you guys don't hold your fire!" At that, several rounds were fired from the bank into the boat.

Gabe yelled at Atherton, "They can't hear you! Hold your fire! Don't shoot him! I'll talk to them."

"Tell them to stop shooting or I'll kill him now. Do you hear me?"

"Yes. Yes, I do hear you. Let me stand up and tell them to hold their fire."

"Okay, but you stand up without your weapon. Do you hear me?"

"I'll do that. Don't shoot." Both men were engaged in a chess match, planning their next moves and buying time. Gabe stood, screaming, "Hold your fire! Don't shoot! It's me, Detective St. John!" The spotlight quickly hit Gabe, who was standing with his hands up while yelling at the cops on the canal bank. "Hold your positions but don't shoot. You got that?"

"Yes, sir," came the response. "We'll stand fast, Detective."

With that done, Gabe turned toward the boat's wheelhouse and, facing Atherton behind the wreckage, said, "Hey, I've done what I said. Now, let Dr. Marchenko go."

"Are you a crazy cop or what? I let him go, and you shoot me as soon as he clears. No way, Detective. Now, why don't you just come on up here with us before I shoot you where you stand." Gabe, thinking that he could do more for Victor by being up on the bridge of the boat, moved toward the ladder.

Atherton pushed Marchenko to the floor and watched Gabe climb the ladder to what was left of the boat's wheelhouse, thinking that his position would be stronger with two hostages. When Gabe entered the cabin, Atherton immediately pushed him against the wall and searched him for weapons. Finding none, he turned him around and noticed the distinctive bulge in Gabe's left-hand shirt pocket from a pack of cigarettes. He removed the pack of Chesterfields from the pocket, and with it came the picture of Leo's that Gabe had kept. "Thanks for the smoke, Officer. I ran out. Can I offer you two one?" With that, Atherton offered the two hostages a cigarette. Both accepted, and as Atherton brought the pack back, he noticed the snapshot. "What do we have here, Detective? A picture of your latest conquest, or is it of your true love?"

"It's nothing, dipshit. It's a picture from the war."

"Well, let's see." Atherton lit the Chesterfield and examined the photo. "What the hell? A bunch of Nazis sitting around a table?"

"It's from Peenemünde, where the Nazis were launching the V-2s at England," Gabe said.

"Peenemünde?" Victor said. "I was there during the war. Can I see it?"

Keeping his cocked pistol trained on St. John, Atherton examined the photograph. Something struck him. He recognized one of the individuals sitting at the table. "What! Who is this, right here?" Atherton was pointing to the white-haired civilian at the table.

Marchenko looked and responded, "I don't know. That man sat in on this meeting. He never spoke a word for two days. He was introduced as a friend to the Reich. That is all that I know. I swear to you."

"That son of a bitch! That traitor! Are you in this picture, Marchenko?"

"Yes, I am right here." He pointed.

"Did you ever see this man again?"

"No," Marchenko replied. "And that was the only time that I ever saw him. Well, except for when he left Peenemünde. When he was boarding the boat for the mainland, I saw him from just outside the entrance to the underground installation. He was wearing the uniform of an SS colonel."

"An SS colonel? Are you sure?"

"Yes. That man was a colonel in the SS. When I saw him, our eyes met for an instant. He then turned to an officer and said something or other. The officer looked at me and then responded to the colonel momentarily. I was afraid, so I returned to my task."

"Why wouldn't he have worn the uniform at that meeting?" Atherton asked.

"I don't know, but I would say that wearing the uniform of an SS colonel would certainly help in traveling. You know, crossing checkpoints and such. Very few of the Wehrmacht would ever challenge an SS colonel, especially that late in the war. Too many were shot for doing just that."

St. John said, "Wait a minute. Do you know this guy? Do you know who he is?"

"Oh yes, Officer, I know who he is. You see, my partner and I were sent here to kill three people who were deemed to be Soviet spies, spies who were stealing information pertaining to the American guidance systems for our ICBMs. That would have been you, Dr. Marchenko, and your two collaborators, the owner of the Optic Company and his assistant, the woman. You, Dr. Marchenko, were supposed to be at that apartment with the other two, but you never showed up, and we had to get out. We could not stay around waiting for you to show. When we returned to Washington, DC, we got reamed out for not hitting you as well. Our supervisor was adamant that we return to this shithole of small-town America and kill you."

"Kill me!" Marchenko exclaimed. "Why would you kill me? I have done nothing but work and aid this country. I am not a Soviet agent. I never trusted or liked that woman who was very close to Mr. Winston. I avoided her at every turn. I never allowed her access to my laboratory. I never associated with her. I just didn't trust her. I am sorry that she is dead, but I did not like her."

"Dr. Marchenko, this entire assignment has come together for me in the last few minutes. I could never understand why we were to kill you. It just never added up. There was never anything I could find within the agency that said that you were a Soviet spy. Many people there had never heard of you, and few had heard your name. But that was it. Nothing that would warrant an agency hit, except, my dear doctor, this man right here." Atherton pointed to the mystery man in the photograph. "He wants you dead."

"Why? I saw him sometime in 1944 at Peenemünde. I haven't seen him since. In fact, I never even thought of this man until I saw the picture."

"I am sure that is the truth, Doctor, but you see, he has never forgotten you. He has never forgotten that you are the only living person who can identify him as an SS colonel. You are the only person who can place him at Peenemünde in 1944 when he was supposed to be running counterinsurgency against the Germans from Zurich. He was an assistant director of the OSS, worked directly under Donovan, and that, my dear doctor, is why you had to be removed. Obviously, at war's end, he found his way over to the Soviets. I would say in Berlin, as that was a city in chaos after the war. The Allied powers were trying to carve it up into their own private fiefdoms. They were so preoccupied with arguing that it would have been easy for the colonel to make contact with the Soviets and cut a deal. He obviously did that, and our agency has been in jeopardy ever since."

A voice came from the canal bank. "You, inside the boat, is everyone all right? Put your weapon down and come out with your hands up, or we're coming in!"

Gabe recognized the voice to be that of Lieutenant George. Gabe and Victor were on the floor, and the assassin joined them to better stay out of the line of fire. Gabe seized this opportunity to speak to Atherton. "I don't know who you are or who you work for, but I do know this, if you kill us or if there are any shots fired in here, you will be carried from this boat and deposited in the morgue. If you put your weapon down and surrender to me, you have a chance. But if you don't, you're a dead man."

Atherton knew that in small-town America, he would be protected from the mob wielding pitchforks and carrying torches and that he would receive a fair trial. He also knew that he would be found guilty and executed. On the other side of the balance, he knew that the agency, and especially the colonel, would never allow him to stand trial. They would play the political card and have him released to the agency or to the federal marshal service whereby he could start life anew with Cheryl. But not before settling some old scores with Colonel Corbin. In Atherton's mind, the pros for surrender won out. "Okay, Detective, you've got a deal. I will surrender. You call the dogs off, and here's my weapon."

As he took the pistol from Atherton, Detective St. John could not believe his luck. There was no one else hurt, and he made the arrest. He cautiously stood up, shouting, "Don't shoot! Don't shoot! He has surrendered. Roy, do you hear me? He has surrendered!"

"Okay, Gabe. Everyone, stand down! Do not shoot!" the lieutenant yelled numerous times.

Gabe helped Victor to his feet and placed Atherton in front of them as they exited the wheelhouse of the Chris-Craft, just in case there might be a trigger-happy cop who didn't understand the orders. Gabe yelled,

"We are coming out! Hold your fire!" They stepped out onto the steps leading down to the deck.

They were met by a sheriff's boat that had been idling in the water at the mouth of the canal. The three men stepped aboard the patrol boat and were ferried to the main street bank where Atherton was taken into custody. Rosary Benedict was there to photograph and write the story as it unfolded. Atherton posed for pictures and gave his name as John Smith of New York. He was whisked away and taken to the station to be booked. Gabe followed the squad car to the station for the booking. Dr. Marchenko was taken to St. Eursala for treatment.

24

I t was nearly four o'clock in the morning when they all arrived at the police station. Atherton was being processed, fingerprinted, and photographed, and all the while, Rosary Benedict was snapping pictures and asking questions of the officers and the lieutenant. She was becoming frustrated and edgy at getting no responses. Also, there was a reporter from the local radio station who had a tape recorder running. He too was trying to get information about the arrest. Finally, Lieutenant George called for attention and stated, "People, we will be holding a news conference at ten o'clock this morning. There will be no information until then. Please leave the station and come back later this morning."

Rose was her usual pissed-off self. Gabe tried to console her. "Rose, we don't know anything about this man. He will be interrogated shortly, and by the time of the news conference, we should have information to share with the media. Now, go home."

"All right, Gabe, I'll go, but you look really beat. Do you want to come home with me?" she asked in a soft, low voice.

"No, Rose, thank you. Another time." Gabe knew that Rose would work on him the rest of the morning trying to get information from him. She was quite talented at that. Sensing that her ploy was not going to work, she stomped out of the station.

Rose was right; Gabe was drained. He approached Roy and said, "I can't function, Roy. I need to get some sleep, and I'm leaving to do that."

"You go, Gabe. We'll take care of it from here. I'll see you for the news conference at ten."

"Thanks, Roy. I'll see you then."

As Gabe got into his car, he thought of Sylvia. He didn't want her to read about the arrest of Zane's murderer in the *Democrat*, so he drove to her house in Northridge. As he approached the house, he saw that the lights were on in the living room. He knew that meant that Sylvia was passed out on the sofa. Not wanting to awaken the children, he knocked softly on the front door, but there was no response, so he tried turning the doorknob, and to his surprise, the front door opened. He went quietly into the house and found Sylvia asleep on the couch, wearing only a see-through short baby doll negligee. He went to her and kissed her gently on the lips, arousing her from her slumber. Sylvia responded to the kiss before she even knew who was kissing her. "Oh, Gabe, I've been wanting to see you so badly."

"I know. I've been very busy," he said this as he worked his way down to her lovely pubic triangle, where he gently began arousing her with his tongue and mouth. Sylvia began making sounds in her throat and responding to his attention to her sacred spot. Gabe buried his face between her legs, sending her into a state of ecstasy. By this time, Gabe needed his own relief as he unzipped his fly to free his tremendous erection.

Sylvia said, "No, upstairs in the bed."

They hastily climbed the stairs to Sylvia's bedroom, where they spent the next two hours. Gabe drifted off to sleep, but at eight thirty, he was awakened by Sylvia giving him his own oral awakening. "God, what a wonderful way to wake up," he told her as she continued her kind work. When she completed the task, he pulled her up to him and kissed her deeply. Gabe then told her of the previous night's events and that Zane's killer was in custody.

She appeared relieved but didn't seem to care about why her husband was murdered or who the suspect was. She only commented, "I'm glad that you caught him, and will I see you later?"

"I've got to be at the station for a ten o'clock news conference. I really don't know about my time today. I'll see you when I can, but it'll be later."

"Well, what do you mean later, Gabe? Do you mean whenever you need a piece of ass?" She got out of bed and headed for the bathroom.

Gabe watched her move, thinking, *My God, she is beautiful.* He responded, "No, Sylvia, I am going to be very busy for the next few days, and I'm not sure when I can get back to see you."

"Okay, Gabe, just when you can. I'll be here," Sylvia said, her head throbbing from the previous night's alcohol.

Gabe lay in the bed a few minutes more until he heard the toilet flush. He then got up and proceeded to the bathroom, meeting Sylvia as she was leaving. He kissed her deeply and applied downward pressure to her shoulders. She sank to her knees and took him once again in her mouth. Gabe showered and dressed, and as he was pulling on his trousers, Sylvia said, "Tell me, Gabe—why did that man shoot Zane? I mean, what was the motive? Was it some kind of lovers' triangle involving his mistress, or was Zane involved with the guy's wife?"

"Neither of those," Gabe said as he lit a cigarette. "Truthfully, we don't know too much, at least I don't. I left the station as they were processing him. They may know more than they did at four o'clock this morning, but I'll find out sometime today." Gabe said nothing about Soviet or American spies. He said nothing about Diane Smith being a KGB agent, Dr. Marchenko, or any of the events of the previous night. He walked to Sylvia's dressing table, where he found an ashtray to stub out his cigarette. He kissed Sylvia deeply, saying, "Thank you for a wonderful night, and I'll see you soon." He glanced back at Sylvia in her naked beauty before leaving the bedroom and heading for the station and the news briefing.

25

Gabe got into his car and had just inserted the key into the ignition when he heard someone call, "Hi, Gabe." He looked in the direction of the voice and saw Eloise Fletcher approaching his car. She was dressed in very short shorts with a T-shirt and stylish leather thong sandals.

Gabe rolled down his window and said, "Good morning, Eloise. Nice to see you."

She came to the car and said, "I've been waiting for you to call me."

"Eloise, honestly, I have been so preoccupied at work that I have not had a chance to do anything else."

"Hum," Eloise murmured as she gestured with her head toward Sylvia's house, "you seem to have time for her."

"Now hold on, Eloise. Sylvia has a direct interest in this case, and I was merely updating her on its latest developments."

"Right, Gabe. I'm waiting to be updated in the same way."

Gabe noticed Eloise's auburn hair falling freely about her shoulders, as well as her ample bosom. He commented, "You're looking very nice this morning."

"I've just gotten out of the shower, Gabe. I'm clean everywhere. The kids are gone, and I would love you to come in the house with me."

"Eloise, I would love to, but I have a very important meeting this morning, and I have to go."

"I read about it in the *Democrat* this morning. Seems you're quite the hero, or at least that's how your little friend at the *Democrat* portrays you."

"Eloise, I've got to go. I'll call you. I promise."

She said with a grin, "You had better." She then turned and walked back to her house, with Gabe watching her every step.

"That," Gabe said to himself, "is all woman."

Gabe arrived at the station just before the news conference. Betty provided him with a cup of coffee, and he carried it onto the podium with Lieutenant George and the chief. The chief started by saying that these heinous crimes had been solved and the perpetrator was now in custody. He bestowed laurels on Lieutenant George and Detective Gabriel St. John for their hard work and perseverance in apprehending the suspect.

The first question came quickly from the reporter from the *Columbus Journal* and related to the murders of Ernie Cobb and the Russian national at St. Eursala. "Were these two murders related to the others?"

The chief said, "I'll turn the questions over to …" At this point, the door to the conference room burst opened, and the FBI came in, with Agent Matthews leading the way to the podium. Three other agents positioned themselves strategically around the room. Matthews leaned over and whispered into the chief's ear. The chief nodded and motioned for Agent Matthews to take the microphone.

"Ladies and Gentlemen, I am Agent Chester Matthews with the Federal Bureau of Investigation, and this news conference is over! Please clear the room at once. The agents will help you exit." There was an immediate uproar from the gathered reporters. They were all yelling questions and demanding answers.

Rosary Benedict was among the loudest, yelling that her readers wanted to know the facts and that Senator McCarthy was now gone. "So why are you still carrying on his witch hunt, Agent Matthews?"

Chester Matthews had two idols. One was the late Senator Joseph McCarthy of Wisconsin and the other was Herbert Hoover. To hear this female reporter referring to one of his idols in a derogatory manner angered him, and he directed one of the agents to escort her out of the room.

Gabe was livid. "Chet! What the fuck are you doing here? This is our news conference. You have no business here. You were ordered to stand down. Do you remember?"

"Sorry, Gabe, but the Bureau has been ordered to take charge of this case. There are national security implications, and I have been ordered to take the case."

"Who ordered you to take the case—our case?"

"My superiors in Washington. Your suspect will be released to federal agents by noon today. He will leave Ohio, and you will never hear of him again. He will be gone. I am not at liberty to provide any more details, nor specific information regarding this case. All that I can say is there are national security implications involved, so please do not ask me any other questions."

"Damn you, Chester, and your Goddamn agency! We take all the risks to bring him into custody, and we get nothing! Nothing except four dead police officers and four unsolved murders. Then you, who were ordered to stand down, parade yourselves in here and take control of the case."

It was apparent to all that Gabe was extremely angry. What no one noticed was Rosary Benedict standing just inside the door to the station conference room, recording the entire exchange among the police and the FBI.

"Detective, I must protest your use of foul and derogatory language toward the Bureau and, by implication, our government. This session has ended!" Chester Matthews stepped down off the podium and headed toward the door with his entourage of agents trailing behind.

The men on the stage, feeling helpless and somewhat defeated, said nothing, except, of course, for Gabe. He screamed, "Fuck the Bureau, fuck the government, and fuck you, you Bible-thumping, McCarthyite, Republican, cocksucking son of a bitch!" With Gabe's frustrations released, he dropped into the nearest chair and lit a cigarette. While Agent Matthews and company exited the room, Rosary Benedict headed to the *Democrat*.

Gabe took a deep pull on the Chesterfield while Chief Cochran was trying to put the pieces of this incident together. He didn't seem to know where to go with it, so he focused on Gabe's outburst. "Gabe, that was uncalled for. You should never have said those things to Agent Matthews, especially your language. Why, those things you said about the FBI and the government and—"

"Chief, blow it out your ass! I'm sick and tired of that pompous bastard trying to run the show by taking over our cases."

"Here now, Detective St. John. You will not talk to me in that—"

Lieutenant George intervened, "Chief, let's go to your office. You both need to cool down, and we can discuss this tomorrow."

Gabe remained seated as the two men left the room. He then stood up to put his cigarette out in the ashtray when Betty walked into the room with a stack of messages for him. "Oh, what a morning. Gabe, what's going on with this case?"

"It's a clusterfuck, Betty. What do you have for me?"

"Well, Eloise Fletcher called twice. Sylvia Winston called," she said as she was dealing out the messages into his hand. "Denise Potts called again. Olivia Rozane called just to make sure you were all right, and Dick Jarvis who works at the Captain's Marina wants to know where the tractor is."

"The tractor—oh, for Christ's sake, the tractor. Betty would you please call him back and tell him that the tractor will be returned to the marina this afternoon. Then call a couple of officers to retrieve the thing from Dr. Marchenko's house and drive it down to the marina."

"Okay, Gabe, and you really look beat. Are you okay?"

"Betty, it's only ten minutes after eleven, and I feel as though I've been here for a week."

"Tell you what, Gabe. What if I make these calls and then we go to my place for lunch and a bit of resting."

Gabe was somewhat taken aback by Betty's proposal. He thought, *Where is this coming from?* He then looked at Betty, and for the first time, he saw a woman and not merely the capable receptionist and dispatcher with whom he had worked every day for the past ten years. He saw perfect breasts and great legs accented by her high heels, and he saw most importantly what he thought to be a friend. "Yeah, okay, Betty, let's do that, but I've got to be back here by one o'clock."

"No problem. I'll be ready in a few minutes. Meet me out front."

They left the station in Gabe's car, heading for Betty's house located on a quiet street in the city's north end. The house was small, with two bedrooms, a living room, small dining room and a kitchen. It was tastefully appointed, and Betty had made it a home. Once inside, Betty stepped out of her heels and padded to the kitchen in her stockings. "Good to get those off for a while," she said as she moved across the carpeted floors. She began to fix two grilled cheese sandwiches, and while they were browning in the skillet, she cut up fresh fruit.

Gabe ate with a relish, and when he finished, he complimented Betty on her culinary skills.

"You don't have anyone to cook for you, do you?"

"Well, no, Betty, I don't, and this lunch was great. Thank you again."

"You need someone to take care of you, Gabe, to support you." She rose from the table and carried the dirty dishes to the sink. "Oh no!" she said as she looked down the front of her skirt. There on the light tan skirt were several dark spots. "Damn, that butter spattered on my skirt. I've got to take care of this right away before it sets and ruins it." With that, she reached around and unfastened the clasp and pulled down the zipper. The skirt fell to the floor around her feet. Betty, standing in her panties, hose, and garter belt, bent over to pick up the skirt, and Gabe's jaw dropped.

She opened the basement door and disappeared for a few minutes to work on her skirt. Gabe lit a Chesterfield and waited for her to return to the kitchen. Then he decided to follow her down into the basement. So, placing the cigarette in the ashtray, he moved toward the basement door. Before he reached the door, Betty was coming up the stairs. She closed the door, and as she turned around, Gabe pinned her against it and kissed her. She reciprocated his embrace with a guttural murmur, saying, "You don't know how long that I have waited for this." They kissed once more, and Gabe let his hands wander over the lower part of her body. His hands slid down the front of her nylon panties, and sensing her dampness, he took her by the hand and headed for her bedroom.

Betty removed her blouse and bra, exposing her lovely shaped breasts with her large nipples. She began to peel her panties down, but Gabe said, "No." She stopped and lay on the bed. He quickly undressed and lay on top of her, working his way down between her thighs. He kissed her through the cover of her panties, applying just enough pressure to cause her to moan softly. Then he removed that last obstacle and buried his face in her. They spent the next hour enjoying each other and making love in the paradise they had discovered.

At twelve thirty, Gabe got out of bed and stood facing Betty, who was enjoying a nap. "We've got to go," he said. She mumbled something about wanting to sleep as she sat up on the edge of the bed, facing Gabe.

She instinctively took his now soft manhood into her mouth. He was erect in an instant. As she finished her oral task, Gabe moaned loudly as he came, but Betty never stopped her motions until Gabe placed his hands on her head, holding it still. Her large doe eyes were looking at him from between his hands, and he said, "Betty, this has been wonderful. I've never experienced these feelings with any other woman before. I, well, we have to get going." With that, an emotionally confused Gabe headed for the shower.

Betty sat back on the bed, drawing her knees up to her chin in a pose of happiness while wondering, *Could he be mine?*

On the drive back, Betty said, "You didn't wear any protection, did you?"

"Huh?" was Gabe's response.

"A rubber! You didn't wear a rubber?"

"Well, uh, no." Gabe was still dealing with strange and confusing feelings.

He shook his head, trying to erase the last two hours and his confusing thoughts about Betty as he walked into the station at a quarter after one. The police station was buzzing with activity. Betty returned to her post behind the counter, and Lieutenant George called Gabe first thing. "Where have you been, boy?"

"I've been to lunch, Roy. What's up?"

"Chester Matthews phoned to give me the heads-up that the feds will be here soon to spring John Smith."

"We expected that, Roy. What's new about that?"

"Well, Gabe, we just want to make this transfer smooth."

"Smooth! What about six homicides on the books of Putnam Landing Police Department? Are they going to give us all the answers to those?"

"I don't expect them to do that, but we will be rid of this guy."

"Rid of him! Rid of him!" Gabe yelled. "What the hell do we tell the citizens of Putnam Landing about six dead people, Roy?"

"We don't. We say it was a federal case, national security interests. That we can't comment."

"Roy, national security in Putnam Landing, what in the hell are you thinking? The *Democrat* and Rosary Benedict will crucify us."

"We'll deal with that."

"Are you out of your mind, Roy? We'll be the laughingstock of the county—of the country, in fact. We have dead cops, three murders, an attempted murder, and a missing assassin. Now you tell me how that is covered up."

"Gabe, I really don't know, and what's more, I don't give a damn. We're rid of the shooter. He's someone else's problem, and we can plead national security, the feds, whatever. I don't care. It's off our plate."

Betty called Lieutenant George and announced that three men were in the lobby to see him. No names were given.

"Gabe, they're here. I'm ordering you to keep your mouth shut and assist in any way possible to make this transfer go smoothly. Do you understand me?"

Gabe bit his tongue and said, "Yes, sir, I do."

The lieutenant picked up the intercom and asked Betty to send them through. The three men, Gabe noticed, were all dressed alike, wearing dark suits, white shirts, dark neckties, and black jodhpur shoes. Two of the three wore dark sunglasses, which they didn't remove. *These guys have all been cut from the same cloth, probably all red, white, and blue,* Gabe thought. The third man was not wearing sunglasses. He was a wiry fellow with a thick accent, who did the talking. The other two, the Foster Grants, as Gabe dubbed them, never spoke a word. The wiry man presented several papers to the chief, saying, "I believe you will find these to be in order for the release of one John Smith who is being held in your jail."

The chief gave the documents a cursory review and passed them to Lieutenant George, saying, "Look these over, Roy, to see if they're in order."

The lieutenant looked at the papers, checking for names and dates. "These don't say to whom we are releasing the prisoner. They just say he's to be released."

"That is all that is needed, Lieutenant," said the man with the heavy accent.

"Not really, sir. You see, we are releasing a suspected murder into your custody, but we don't know who you are. We don't know where the suspect is going. For all we know, you men are part of his gang, or you will just turn him loose once you get him out the door. I'm afraid that we will need names, as well as the jurisdiction that we are releasing the suspect to, the suspected murderer. I am sure you understand, sir, that we need this to protect ourselves and our department."

"Lieutenant, you will produce this man and release him to my custody immediately! Is that clear?"

"Whoa, my friend, you aren't in the Reich anymore. You are in small-town America where we do business differently. You provide us with the names and his destination, and we will turn him over to you, and you can goosestep him all the way back to Washington for all I care, but we follow procedure here—and no names, no prisoner."

The two Foster Grants bristled. They separated, taking up locations in different parts of the room. Gabe, sensing there could be an altercation, stood up, loosened his sports coat, and moved toward the door so as to have a shot at one or both of them if it came to that. The heavily accented man said, "Yes, of course, Lieutenant. How clumsy of me." With that, he removed a fountain pen from his pocket and filled in the blanks for the lieutenant. He returned the pen to his pocket.

Roy George checked the document and said, "Bring up the prisoner."

Gabe noticed that the two men in sunglasses had relaxed their stance, so he opened the office door and said to the nearest officer, "Go down and get Smith and make sure he's cuffed."

"Yes, sir, Detective, right away." With that, the officer went down the stairs to the cells to get John Smith.

While waiting in the chief's office for their prisoner, Chief Cochran said, "I'm sorry for the delay, gentlemen, but you must understand our situation."

"Yes, we do understand, and we are very sorry for any misunderstanding. Please accept my sincere apologies."

There was a knock on the door, and the jailer entered with Atherton in chains. Atherton immediately recognized Berger, the colonel's aid, as the heavily accented spokesman. His manacles were removed by the jailer, and Berger said, "Thank you, gentlemen. We must now be on our way." They left the office and the station and drove away in a large Lincoln.

"Jesus! What just happened?" Gabe said.

"I don't know, sir, but you guys just released the prisoner to Otto Hohenzollern, holy Roman emperor who died during the first crusade."

"What?" Lieutenant George exclaimed.

"Well, yes, sir," the young jailer went on, "unless that guy's name is for real, which I doubt, you just released the prisoner to a man who has been dead for over eight hundred years."

"That son of a bitch," Roy murmured.

27

The three men and Atherton were headed for the Columbus Airport. Atherton was not sure what to expect from this ride because they had failed on their mission and because the colonel did not like loose ends. The thought crossed his mind that this could be his last ride. The Lincoln could turn off on some side road, one shot in the back of the head from one of the sunglass-wearing goons, his body kicked out of the car, and that would be it. The jailer in Putnam Landing had returned his .38 and holster, which he kept his hands on as they proceeded west on Route 40, but he quickly dismissed that thought as being too obvious. A man just released from jail found shot on desolate road. Nope, wouldn't happen. Nevertheless, he kept the pistol close to him and his eye on the other three men.

Atherton lit a cigarette as Hans said, "We have a four o'clock flight out of Columbus to Dulles International. The colonel wants to see you in the morning at ten o'clock sharp for a debriefing. Is that clear?"

Thomas thought, *You fucking Kraut. You are still in the Third Reich.* He took a drag on his cigarette saying, "Yeah, okay, Berger, I'll be there. Tell the colonel not to worry."

"Very good," was Berger's response. Thomas thought, *I want to talk with that traitor bastard too and settle a score.*

The flight to Washington, DC, was uneventful. At the airport, Atherton left the other three men, as his car was in a different parking lot from theirs. He got into the Jaguar, and the smell of leather was overpowering. He loved it. That wonderful engine roared to life, and Atherton was on his way. His first stop was for food. He was starving. He had not eaten since noon, and that was jail food. So he pulled off at Jake's Café. He entered the café to find a few people, mostly locals, he thought, who were drinking at the bar and a few others scattered at the tables. He sat down and ordered a beer and food. Atherton then asked the waitress if there was a phone. She pointed to the rear of the restaurant where he found two phone booths. He deposited a dime and dialed. His first call was to TWA to schedule two seats to Rio de Janeiro for the following day. His second call was Cheryl's number. When she answered, he said, "Cheryl, listen to me, just listen. Pack a bag and come to my apartment at twelve o'clock tomorrow. There will be a key above the door on the ledge, so you can get in. Let yourself in and wait for me. We have a four o'clock flight, TWA, to Rio, where I want to spend the rest of my life with you. Do you understand that?"

"Yes," she responded breathlessly. "Oh, Thomas, I do love you, and I have some news for you."

"Great, tomorrow then at my apartment." With that, he hung up.

Atherton finished his meal and a second beer, paid the check, and left the restaurant. Leaving the parking lot, he pointed the Jag toward Virginia and the home of the agency's director of operations, George McNaulty. McNaulty was anything but a hands-on director. While he was responsible for all field operations, he remained aloof from the agents and their work. Thomas figured it was so that he would be able to plead maximum deniability in the event of a badly blown assignment. He had met him one time when McNaulty had attended a debriefing session on a South American assignment. Atherton had not been inspired with this man who sat in the shadows of the room and never spoke. When the session ended, McNaulty quickly vacated the room with his three assistants. Atherton remembered chasing after him and loudly calling his name for all to hear. McNaulty stopped, pivoted, and gave Thomas an icy glare. "Sir," Atherton continued in the same loud voice, "I just wanted to say how pleased we are to have the director of operations attend our debriefing. It is not too often that we have the pleasure of having our supervisory officers attend and share with us the benefits of their experiences and to hear their comments on a job well done." Director McNaulty continued his glare, then mumbled something, pivoted back toward the exit, and was gone.

Thomas smiled as he lit a cigarette. As he approached Alexandria, he downshifted the Jag to rein it in to allow for the increased traffic. As he did so, he could hear the throaty rumble of the exhaust. "Wow, next to a good woman, that is the best sound ever." He turned on the outskirts of the city and wound his way through a residential neighborhood, driving slowly to read the house numbers. At last, he came to it, a large Georgian brick situated at the last on at least five acres of ground. "Thank you, Scottie," Atherton commented to himself. Scottie was his friend in the personnel section who had provided Thomas with information on Director McNaulty after their run-in at the debriefing session. Atherton had looked over the information and then had shredded it to protect all parties. He parked the Jag and surveyed the premises. He could not see any security on the parameters, but who knew what may be inside.

He proceeded up the long sidewalk and rang the doorbell. A woman in her fifties, dressed as a maid, answered the door. Atherton identified himself and asked for Mr. McNaulty. The woman asked that he step into the hall and wait while she summoned him.

"Who is it, Louisa?" came a female voice from the opposite end of the hall. A woman appeared, walking down the hall from what Atherton thought must be the kitchen. She was attired in shorts and a T-shirt, barefooted. In her mid to late thirties, she was statuesque and put together, Atherton thought as she approached him.

"I'm Mrs. McNaulty. Can I help you?"

"Well, ma'am, I'm here to see your husband, if you please."

"He's on a phone call, but he should be here presently."

"Thank you, ma'am," he said as she turned and retreated down the hall. "If I can help you, please let me know," she said over her shoulder.

Jeez, Atherton thought, *old George has a fox for a wife.*

Director McNaulty came down the hall and asked, "How may I help you, sir?" Then he recognized Atherton and said in a raised voice,

"What are you doing here and how did you find me? How do you know where I live?"

"Sir, please, I have something to talk to you about concerning our national security. Can we please talk in private?"

"This better be good, mister, or you'll be on the street in the morning."

"Please, Director McNaulty!"

"All right, come this way." The director led Atherton out of the hall, through a room, and into his study.

Once in a secure location, Atherton related the entire Putnam Landing operation to the director. He stressed the urgency that Colonel Corbin had placed on the entire operation and that Dr. Marchenko, along with Zane Winston and Diane Smith, had to be eliminated, then how they had to return to Putnam Landing to finish the job with Dr. Marchenko. Director McNaulty looked wide-eyed at Atherton and said, "What are you talking about? Where is Putnam Landing? What operation? I have absolutely no knowledge of this. What was Corbin thinking?"

"Sir, I'm just telling you what our orders were, as well as the urgency."

"Mr. Atherton, I'm telling you right now that this was a rogue operation and not sanctioned in any way by me or the agency."

"Yes, sir, I've arrived at that conclusion on my own." Atherton went on to explain his arrest on the boat and the photograph from Peenemünde. He pointed out the man in civilian clothes at the table and explained the photo bona fides.

McNaulty took the picture and examined it with a jeweler's loop. "My God!" he exclaimed. "That's Corbin."

"Yes, sir, it is."

The director stood up and told Atherton to wait for him. He disappeared into a small room off the study, where he remained for about forty-five minutes. When he came out, he went to the door of the study and yelled to Louisa, "We want a pot of strong coffee and a tray of sandwiches."

"Yes, sir, I'll have them in a few minutes."

"Also, tell Mrs. McNaulty not to bother us or interrupt us for the rest of the night. Do you understand that?"

"Yes, sir, I do. I will tell her," Louisa replied as she left the kitchen.

McNaulty turned to Thomas and explained, "We are going to be joined by a few other company men. We will wait to proceed until they arrive."

While they waited, the director confided in Atherton that Colonel Corbin had been on the agency's radar for some time. "I can tell you this now, as you have come to us not only with your own suspicions but the proof. Nevertheless, I will expect you to maintain complete confidentiality regarding this matter."

"I understand that, sir, and I will never divulge anything regarding this discussion to anyone." The director didn't acknowledge Atherton's reply. Thomas then proceeded to relate to Director McNaulty the events surrounding his father's death in Zurich during the war. He ended their lengthy recap by saying, "Now that I know that the colonel was a German spy, I'm convinced that my father's death was not a suicide but a murder, a murder at the hands of Colonel Benjamin Corbin and his Nazi collaborators."

"That may be very well true, Mr. Atherton, and we will consider that in our deliberations this evening." Their conversation ended with a knock on the door and Louisa showing three gentlemen into the study.

There were no introductions, but the three greeted the director on a first-name basis. They were all dressed in expensive suits and carried briefcases, which they placed on the table in the study. Atherton recognized one of the men only as a person he had seen on several occasions in the halls of the CIA building. He didn't know his name or position. The other two he had never laid eyes on before. They looked him over for several seconds, and then, looking at the director, one asked if it was all right to speak freely about the matter at hand. "Yes, gentlemen, by all means. This agent approached me with the evidence, so speak freely."

They took seats at the table, opened their briefcases, and began passing out papers. Atherton was omitted from this process. The nameless men and McNaulty pored over the documents, as well as the photograph from Peenemünde. They posed questions among themselves and to Thomas. They constructed timelines and charts, and by three o'clock in the morning, they had pretty much arrived at their answer. Corbin was a Soviet mole, as was his aid, Berger. From what Atherton could gleam from the meeting, the accusations stopped there. He was asked to leave the room at three thirty while they conducted a sensitive matter. That suited Thomas because after a night of drinking Louisa's coffee, he had to use the bathroom. He moved down the hall toward the restroom when the study door opened behind him and a man passed him and darted into the room ahead of him. "Damn," he whispered, "I've got to go." And with that, he climbed the stairs in search of the upstairs facility. As he was finishing and zipping his fly, the bathroom door opened, and there, wearing only a brief pair of panties, entered Mrs. McNaulty. Atherton immediately tried to zip his pants but found the task impossible in light of his tremendous hard-on. Mary Lou looked at it, pulled her panties off, and dropped to her knees in front of him.

Atherton began to protest when she said, "Be quiet, you fool. We don't have much time." He clammed up, and she clamped his hard-on between her lips. After a few seconds, she stood up and walked to the bathtub, where she bent over with her head down into the tub and stood with her feet slightly apart. Atherton followed and inserted himself into her back door, thrusting deeply into her warm, wet, womanly spot. He came like a fire hose, almost dropping to the floor. Mrs. McNaulty turned around and took his now flaccid penis into her mouth, bobbing back and forth on it for a few more times. She stood up and said, "Thank you, Thomas. I will now be able to get some sleep." Smiling, she exited the bathroom, sans panties, and disappeared. Atherton remained in the bathroom for a few seconds, trying to figure it all out but to no avail. He zipped his fly and returned to the group, only to find them leaving the McNaulty house. Each filed past Atherton without so much as a glance in his direction.

As the director closed the door when the last man left, Atherton commented, "What a friendly group of guys."

Director McNaulty looked at Thomas and said, "Mr. Atherton, may I have a bit more of your time in my study?"

"Yes, sir, I have time." They reentered the study, and McNaulty motioned for Thomas to sit at the table. He explained that Corbin had to be dealt with in such a way as to not call attention to the agency through press involvement.

"Do you understand what I am saying, Mr. Atherton?"

"I do, sir, know exactly what you're saying."

"Fine, fine. Now, what time is your meeting with Colonel Corbin? Ten o'clock, didn't you say?"

"Yes, sir, at his house."

"Well, that has been changed. Your meeting will now be here at eleven o'clock. The colonel has been notified that a car will call for him at ten. I took the liberty of explaining to the group about your father and Zurich. They thought you might take on the task of eliminating our problem in the car on your way here for the meeting."

"Director McNaulty, I was going to request that I be the one to get him. I want to do that for my father."

"I thought so. Now, what you must do is take care of the problem before the car gets into this subdivision. Is that clear?"

"Yes, sir, I will do that. I wish to settle the score for my father."

"Very well, Mr. Atherton. The car will pick you up at nine thirty this morning, and here, this is for your use." McNaulty handed Atherton a 1911 Colt .45, along with a silencer. "Use this, as there is less room for error, and it's clean. The serial number has been removed." Atherton took the .45. He ejected the magazine and examined the rounds. They were hollow points. He replaced the magazine and checked the chamber where he found the round. "It has been cleaned, oiled, and sighted in by the armory. I think you will find it ready to go, Mr. Atherton."

"Yes, sir, I love these slab-sided .45s. They have served our nation well."

"Yes, they have, Mr. Atherton, and now, if you don't mind, you have your instructions, and I have to get some sleep."

"Yes, sir." *I bet you do,* Atherton thought, *next to a woman who I just nailed in your upstairs bathroom.*

He turned the key to the D-type Jaguar and lit a cigarette.

28

I t was six thirty in the morning as Atherton pulled onto the highway
for his return trip. Even though he had been up all night, the
sandwiches and the strong coffee and his encounter with Mary
Lou McNaulty left him feeling alert and blissful. He also felt hungry,
so he stopped at an all-night diner for breakfast. He had two and a half
hours before he could get into his bank, which gave him time to reflect
on the night. The part that aroused his suspicions was that no names
were given of the men at the meeting, and then ending from which he
was excluded. "Why exclude me at that point?" he asked himself over
and over. A little voice in his head was trying to tell him something, but
it wouldn't register clearly.

He paid his check and left the diner. It was nearly eight thirty, and
the morning traffic into DC was miserable. The Jag inched along in
places and ran at thirty miles an hour in others. He knew that he had
to be at his bank by nine o'clock to get his money out in cash and return
to his apartment. Then it hit him. *Oh Christ!* he thought aloud. *If the
colonel is scheduled for removal, what about his organization? What about
him? What about the other eight?* Carl was already taken care of, so what
about him? Especially him, as he was the one who had positively exposed
Colonel Corbin. He knew too much; as Carl had said, they could not
trust his silence. That long meeting from which he was excluded at the
end of the night, what was that about? Even his encounter with Mrs.

McNaulty, was that part of their plan to keep him busy and keep his mind off what they were discussing? The more that he thought about it, the more he thought, *No, I'm all right. They will use me, and the rest of us, somewhere else in the agency. I'm okay.* Atherton tried to convince himself.

He entered the bank at exactly nine o'clock and sat down with one of the bankers. "Mr. Bergan, I am on a very narrow timeline, and I must have your complete attention and cooperation."

"Yes, sir, Mr. Atherton. How can I help you?"

"I must have access to my safety deposit box now."

"Sure, sir. Follow me." Atherton followed the bank officer down to the safety deposit box area. Atherton was carrying a large satchel-type briefcase as he followed Bergan to the desk of the woman in charge of that area.

"Marg," Bergan said, "this is Mr. Atherton. He needs to get into his safety deposit box."

"Certainly," Marg responded. "I know Mr. Atherton and will be glad to help him." They went through the necessary protocol, and Marg extracted Thomas's box from the vault. She showed him into a small phone-booth-sized room and left him alone. Atherton sat about opening the large box where his total life savings of $92,357 resided. He quickly transferred the cash into his satchel and left the bank.

Atherton drove the few blocks to his apartment. He ran into the building and down the long corridor to his apartment. Once inside, he placed the satchel on the table, picked up a tablet, and wrote a note to Cheryl. "My love, if I am not here by 2:20 p.m., you are to take a taxi to Dulles. Go to the TWA counter and pick up your ticket to Rio de Janeiro. It will be $400. Take this briefcase with you. I advise you to count out the money quietly in the cab before you arrive at the airport. Do not wait for me past 2:20 p.m. If I am not here, go, and I will join you later. Love, Thomas. P. S. Cheryl, you may be in danger if I am not here. Do not wait! Leave!"

At 9:30 exactly, there was a knock on the apartment door. Atherton opened the door to a man in a dark suit wearing sunglasses. The man said, "Mr. Atherton, your car is downstairs, sir."

"Fine, I'll be right with you." Atherton placed the note on top of the bag of money and followed the man down to the car.

Thomas was shown into the back seat on the driver's side of the Lincoln. The man occupied the front passenger's seat next to the driver. They proceeded to the colonel's brownstone, where they picked him up at ten fifteen and began the trip to Director McNaulty's house in Alexandria. The colonel was talkative. The two in the front seat said nothing.

After they had been driving for thirty minutes, Atherton asked the colonel about his father. "Yes, I do remember him well, son. A terrible tragedy, him jumping out of that window."

"Well, you see, Colonel, I'm of the belief that he was thrown out of that window, either by you or your Nazi counterparts."

"What are you talking about?"

"We have a picture, Colonel, a picture of you at Peenemünde during the war. A picture that shows you attending a conference with other high-ranking Nazis."

"What are you talking about, Atherton?"

"I'm talking about you as a Nazi collaborator, Colonel. I'm talking about you as authorizing a rogue operation to kill the only person that could identify you as a spy. I am talking about you as a Soviet agent who colluded with the Russians to murder Dr. Marchenko in Putnam Landing, Ohio. You, Colonel, are a spy and a traitor to your country, and you have been since the war. That's what this ride is about."

"Well, let me tell you, boy, your father was merely a casualty of war. He came to see me about his contract. He showed up late and overheard my conversation with my Gestapo handler. We heard him leave and watched him walk away from the building and cross the street. Whatever happened after that, I do not know. The fool wound up dead, I do know that, but I had nothing to do with his death, and that's the truth."

"Well, Colonel, what about today? What about the Soviets?"

"You fool, they have the system that will take over the world. We will have peace and security under their rule. I should have been appointed director of the CIA when it was founded, but that stupid Truman appointed that cold fish Bedle Smith. Then that queer was named after him. He and his pipe-smoking queer brother are running this country. Ike doesn't have a clue."

Atherton leveled the .45 and squeezed the trigger. The colonel's head exploded with one round. "You Commie son of a bitch!" were Atherton's last words. He never heard the second shot, the one that tore through his brain, killing him instantly.

The man in the front seat put his pistol into the holster as the Lincoln sped toward the Maryland scrapyard. Once there, the two men left the car, got into another waiting car, and drove away. The Lincoln was crushed into a four-by-four cube of steel. Within two months of the colonel's demise, his wife, an otherwise fit and healthy woman, suffered a fatal heart attack. Berger and his aide were struck by a hit-and-run driver and killed. The driver was never found. Federal agents tore apart the brownstone and found a Soviet radio, the same as the one found in Diane Smith's apartment in Putnam Landing, along with codes and the codebook, as well as piles of other incriminating evidence against the colonel. He was a spy and a traitor.

At 11:40, Cheryl arrived at Atherton's apartment. She let herself in with the key he had left above the door. She immediately spied the briefcase and the note. Reading it, her concern for Thomas's safety rose, but she kicked off her heels and put her legs up on the sofa to wait for him. By two o'clock, she was frantic, with tears welling up in her eyes. At 2:20, she gathered up her suitcase and the bag of money and went down to the street to hail a taxicab. As she got into the cab, she thought, *I'll have to wait to tell him that I'm carrying his child. I'll see him in Rio.* And with that, Cheryl was never heard from again.

Detective St. John left the Putnam Landing police station shortly after Atherton's release. He was feeling frustrated and angry at letting a murderer walk. "Where's the justice?" he said to Betty as he paused at her work area on his way out to his car.

"Gabe, why don't you stop by my place and take a shower and a rest. I'll be home by five thirty to fix us dinner, and we can just relax and talk."

"That sounds wonderful, Betty, but I've got some things I must do between now and tonight. I'll take a rain check." Gabe meant every word he said. The thought of a relaxing evening and a nice meal with her was just what he needed. She had been on his mind for the entire afternoon.

She seemed a bit disappointed but said, "Fine, will you call me later?"

"You can count on it," he said with a longing in his voice and a loving smile.

Gabe wanted to see Olivia Rozane to tell her that she wouldn't need her Browning, as the threat was gone. He wanted to stop by Sylvia's to explain what had happened with her husband's killer and to break off their relationship once and for all.

He pulled up in the driveway at the Rozane house and rang the bell of the side door. Ms. Snead promptly opened the door, saying, "Detective, nice to see you. Mrs. Rozane is in her sitting room. She will be pleased that you stopped by."

Gabe, caught off guard by his reception, replied, "Thank you, Ms. Snead. Nice to see you as well."

The housekeeper showed him upstairs to Olivia's quarters and announced him. "Gabe, what a pleasant surprise for an old woman."

"Hello, Olivia. I hope I'm not interrupting your afternoon, but I need to speak with you."

"No, my boy, it's fine. Evelyn, please leave us."

The housekeeper turned and left the room. "I've been reading about your exploits in the *Democrat*, Gabe. It sounds as though you've done a wonderful job apprehending the murderer of Zane and that woman." Rosary Benedict had written the entire episode in the police station, and the *Democrat* had printed it on the front page. The entire story was there—from the problems at the press conference to the angry arguing afterward to the release of the prisoner to federal authorities.

Gabe had not seen a newspaper, and when Olivia pushed her copy in front of him, he said, "Oh my God, how did she get this? Chet Matthews will be livid." Deep down, Gabe was pleased.

Olivia lit a cigarette and listened as Gabe gave her a rundown of Atherton's capture and subsequent release. At the end, he said, "Olivia, I just wanted you to know that you are no longer in danger."

She chuckled, pulling the Browning 9 mm out of her desk drawer. "You mean I won't need this?"

"Well, no, not for the present, but you might want to keep it close by."

"Don't worry, it's never too far from me, Gabe."

Gabe stood up, saying, "Olivia, I have several more stops to make, so I must leave."

She bade him goodbye, saying, "Stop back any time for a chat and stay for dinner."

Gabe pulled into the driveway at Sylvia Winston's house. Her children were riding bicycles on the sidewalk with the Fletcher children. He waved to them as he approached the front door. Sylvia greeted him wearing a pair of short shorts and a T-shirt, barefooted. She was carrying a gin and tonic and said, "God, it's so good to see you, Gabe. I need to tell you some things."

She walked into the living room, halting only to ask him if he wanted a gin, to which he replied, "Yes." She went to the kitchen to refresh her drink and fixed Gabe one. She returned with the drinks and dropped down on the sofa close to Gabe. Gabe lit a cigarette and took a pull of the gin and tonic. He then recounted for Sylvia the day's events.

She put up her hand to stop him, lit a cigarette, and said, "I know. I read the damn news, but listen to my news. After you left the other morning, I received a telephone call from a bank in Switzerland. Get that, a call from Switzerland. Some guy from a bank called Credit Suisse. Well, anyway, this guy said that his bank had a client who wanted to buy the company for $4 million. I couldn't believe what I was hearing. I said, 'Sold!' They wired me $1 million—as he said, a good faith down payment. Gabe, do you know what this means? With Zane's insurance money and this, I will have over $6 million. Gabe, we can do anything we want to."

"Wait a minute, Sylvia! Wait! You're selling the plant from under those employees, some of whom have spent their lives working there? What will happen to them?"

She looked at him quizzically. Tilting her head slightly, she said, "What are you talking about?"

"Sylvia, our government will take Dr. Marchenko and a select few others to another secure research facility. They could never allow him to leave, knowing what he knows. The rest of the employees will be put on the street. The plant will close in Putnam Landing."

"Well, why would they do that, Gabe? It's a perfectly good plant. Wouldn't they just continue on?"

"No, Sylvia, it doesn't work that way. This plant will be closed."

"Well, anyway, darling." Gabe cringed at her use of that word. "We can go anywhere in the world that we want. We will have the money to do anything and live anywhere." She nuzzled close to Gabe, placing her hand on his thigh and rubbing it. She leaned forward to put out her cigarette and then returned to Gabe and kissed him. Gabe responded to her touches and her kiss and somehow found the strength to stop her. This was not an easy feat to accomplish with Sylvia.

"This isn't going to work, Sylvia, this relationship between us."

"What do you mean? It seems to be working just fine."

"That's the thing, Sylvia. What works is the sex we have. Nothing else."

"Gabe," she said, standing up in front of him and quickly disrobing, "we have this. This is yours to do with whatever you have the need to do and whenever you want to do it."

He sat staring at this raven-haired beauty, admiring her firm breasts, her flat stomach, her lovely pubic area mounted with thick, dark hair, and her shapely legs and feet. *I do love her, but do I like her?* As he sat trying to sort out his feelings, she dropped to her knees and unzipped his pants. She extracted his fully extended penis and began gently licking its shaft before engulfing him in her mouth. She moved her head up and down while using her tongue to brush across its tip. Gabe came in a moaning climax. Sylvia pulled her head back, swallowed hard, and returned to finish her duties.

After a few seconds, she stood up and got dressed. "That's what we have, Gabe, and that's what we will have every day of our lives from this day forward." Gabe repositioned himself on the couch beside her. Sylvia lit a Philip Morris, and as she exhaled with a wicked smile on her lips, she said, "I always like a smoke after I eat."

"But, Sylvia, don't you see? This is all." At that moment, the front door burst open to the din and chattering of four children.

Gabe stood up, saying, "Thank you, Mrs. Winston, for your time and hospitality. I will be in touch."

Gabe walked to the door as Sylvia said, "I'll be expecting to hear from you, Detective."

Gabe lit a Chesterfield as he drove home. All he wanted to do now was talk with Leo and tell him the crucial part his photograph had played in the case. Then he wanted a long, hot shower and a strong gin and tonic. He entered the house but did not find Leo. He called his name, but there was no response. As he went to the kitchen, he saw a note on the table. "Gabe, I found an apartment over near the new high school. I have returned to Chicago to get the rest of my things out of storage. I will see you in a few days. Thanks! Leo."

Well, okay, so much for Leo. Now, how about that shower, he thought. Following the shower, he wrapped a towel around himself and returned to the kitchen to fix a gin and tonic. He lit a cigarette and took a deep drink of the gin. "God," he said, "that is so good." Gabe was headed for the bedroom to get dressed as the doorbell rang. Since he had not been home too much over the last few days, he thought maybe it was Leo returning early. He walked to the living room, put his cigarette out, and, carrying his gin, opened the door. There, standing in her own beauty was Eloise Fletcher. "Well, what the hell are you doing here, Eloise?" he asked.

She quickly stepped inside, saying, "You haven't called me, so I just decided to call on you. Gee, I like that you're dressed for the occasion."

"Why are you so dressed up?" Eloise was wearing a khaki skirt with a white blouse and tan and white high heels with stockings. "Where have you been?" He turned for her response to find the skirt on the floor and the blouse coming off.

She followed him into the living room, saying, "My husband won't be home anytime soon, the kids are seen to, and I've been to an interview for a part-time job at the country club." The blouse and bra were discarded as she followed Gabe to the couch. They made it no further, spending their time in bliss until seven o'clock when Eloise began gathering her clothes for the drive home. She found everything but her panties. Gabe hadn't removed the garter belt and hose, just the panties. They were nowhere to be found. Eloise finally said, "Don't worry about them. I'll go home, take a shower, and put on a clean pair anyway." And with that, she was out the door and gone.

Gabe's head was swimming—too many women but no commitment. Was this how it was supposed to be? As he took a second shower, Betty's image reappeared and would not leave.

These feelings were new to Gabe. He did not understand them, nor was he sure that he even wanted to. He had never been exposed to such an emotional roller coaster. Perhaps, if his mother had not died at his young age, she would have helped him through. She had left him at an age when children, especially boys, need their mother the most—the critical teenage years when a mother's voice is crucial for taming a boy and helping him channel his testosterone-fueled desires into more socially accepted actions. His father was no help, living as he did in alcohol-fueled rages. Frequently, Gabe and his mother were the victim of his rages.

He had friends, but he didn't know how to nurture or to love. He had always had women, and he enjoyed their company, but the next morning, he made sure that they parted company. If one of them began to pursue him or push too hard for more than he could give to her, he never saw her again. *Possibly*, he thought, *that's why I'm drawn to married women. They're safer. With them, there's no talk of anything beyond the moment. They're bored with their lives, and I'm horny, and it's worked—until Betty, that is. Why is she different? Why do I find myself running to her, and why am I so mixed up?*

He woke up on Saturday morning to the doorbell. He was still on the living room couch, where he had dropped following his second shower. The towel that had been around him was gone, following a night of too many gins. The doorbell continued blaring until he responded. With the towel wrapped around him, he answered the door. It was Betty standing in shorts and sandals and a T-shirt, carrying a bag of groceries. "Betty, what are you doing here?"

"I thought I would stop by and fix our breakfast."

"Oh, yeah, come in," Gabe replied as the towel began to drop from his waist.

She observed this and said, "Umm, am I interrupting?"

"No, no, I took shower last night and just sat on the couch, had a few drinks, and the next thing I knew, you were ringing the doorbell. That's it."

"Why don't you get dressed, and I'll start our breakfast."

He went into the bedroom to dress, feeling a warm, pleasant glow as he slipped into a pair of shorts and a T-shirt.

Betty had stepped out of her sandals and was busy frying bacon, making coffee, and slicing a cantaloupe. She had already set the table, and as she set the melon on the table, she said, "Why don't you start on this. It will be a while before the rest of the breakfast is ready. The coffee is almost fixed." He sat down and ate the melon down to the rind. He had not eaten any food the night before and was starving.

When they had finished eating, Gabe thanked her for fixing the food and said, "Let's go into the living room with our coffee." He led the way to the couch, where he lit a cigarette and took a sip of the strong coffee Betty had made. She followed and sat down next to him. They drank their coffee and talked about the station and some of its people. They talked about the prisoner release and joked and laughed about families.

Then Betty turned serious. She looked directly into Gabe's eyes and said, "Gabriel St. John, I am helplessly and hopelessly in love with you, and I honestly think that I have been since the first day I laid eyes on you."

Gabe stared at her. He had heard similar professions of love before but never from Betty and never as deeply expressed. Gabe was speechless for a few seconds. He then lit another cigarette and said, "Betty, I have not been able to get you out of my mind since our lunch the other day. You're just always there. All the other women pale in comparison to you. You're the one, Betty. I too love you." He had finally said it, those words; he couldn't help himself. He was in love with Betty. She excused herself to go to the bathroom. Gabe returned to the kitchen to pour another cup of coffee. He returned to the couch, lit a Chesterfield, and thought, *What have I just said?* But he couldn't deny it. He did love Betty.

She returned from the bathroom after about twenty minutes. She was naked and carrying her clothes. She dropped them neatly on a chair and curled up next to Gabe on the sofa. They began kissing, and Gabe was massaging her large nipples. She reached for him, but he stood up momentarily to remove his clothes. When he returned to her, she had lain back on the couch and placed her legs back as far as she could so that her toes were almost touching the arm of the couch behind her. Gabe immediately went to work with his mouth, and in a few moments, she screamed with ecstasy. Then he entered her, and once again, she screamed and went to another reality. Gabe withdrew from her and said, "Oh Jesus, Betty, you are the best that I've been with." She sat up and bent down to his lap, taking his penis into her mouth and bathing it with her mouth and tongue. He loved it.

She sat up, looked at him, and said, "That was wonderful. Thank you, Gabe, but you still didn't use a rubber, and this is still a dangerous week of the month for me."

"Using a rubber for sex is like smoking a cigarette with a filter. No taste, no feel, no anything. I don't use them."

"Just know this—this is my terrible time of the month."

"Betty, I don't care. I love you, and I want to marry you. Will you be my wife?"

"Yes, Gabe, I will be your wife." They talked for a while about the future, but then Betty stood up and said, "I've got to go, but call me later. We have a lot of plans to make."

Gabe watched her dress and followed her to the front door, still naked. He took her in his arms and kissed her deeply. She told him that she loved him and left the house.

Gabe returned to the couch and dropped. He reached for a cigarette. As he leaned back, he became aware of Betty's womanly aroma on the sofa, as well as on him. Her sweet, musky scent permeated the entire room. He said, "What a woman I've found, and she'll be my wife." He was a happy man.

32

By Labor Day 1956, the old city was returning to its normal quiet and bucolic self. The murders of Zane Winston and Diane Smith and the arrest and release of John Smith, a.k.a. Thomas Atherton, were moving to the back of the townspeople's minds.

Betty was in her first trimester of pregnancy, and she jokingly said to Gabe, "You had better make an honest woman out of me before this kid has graduated from high school."

"I would marry you today. Let's go find Monsignor."

Sylvia Winston completed the sale of Winston Optics to the Swiss firm. She sold her house and was leaving for Phoenix by that October. She and Gabe never talked about their future or anything else ever again. At some level, they both knew that all they ever had between them was great sex and that a lasting relationship would never work.

Strangely enough, Gabe ran into Eloise Fletcher at the Grill, where they were both buying groceries. She was dressed in that same khaki skirt and two-tone heels, which conjured up pleasant memories for Gabe. She told him, "You will never believe what has happened. My husband has been offered a sizable promotion, and we are moving to Chicago. We will be relocating there after the holidays." Gabe offered his congratulations to the husband and stated that he would miss seeing her. "Gabe, we had wonderful times together, but that was it. I will always remember them." Gabe nodded and wished her good luck. Eloise walked out of the Grill and out of Gabe's life.

CHAPTER

33

November 14, 1956, was the day Gabe and Betty were married at Holy Rosary Church. Gabe had no relatives and only a few close friends to invite. Leo was his best man. Betty too had no family to speak of, just her mother, a few aunts and uncles, and a smattering of cousins. Most of the attendees were fellow police officers. Olivia Rozane attended and presented the happy couple with a sizable check and keys to her house in Key West, Florida, for their use as long as they desired. Also at the reception, Lieutenant George and Chief Cochran informed Gabe that he was to fill Roy George's position when Chief Cochran retired on January 2, and the lieutenant would be named chief of police. It was a done deal, they told him, already approved by the city council.

Gabe and Betty spent their time in Key West luxuriating on the beach and in each other. Gabe had never been happier in his life. They returned to Ohio relaxed and tanned and went to housekeeping in Betty's house. Before they had left, Gabe offered to rent his house to Leo if he could arrange it with the manager of the apartment complex where he was planning on moving. Leo jumped at the chance and moved in while they were on their honeymoon.

The bodies of the two KGB agents, Yuri and Diane, were finally claimed by two Russian diplomats and transported back to Russia for burial. In mid-January, a badly decomposed and eaten body surfaced at the boat dock at Tim's Bar and Grill on the river. Gabe instinctively knew that it was the remains of the second assassin, which Dr. Eli's autopsy proved. He removed a .38 slug from the upper right quadrant of the remains, and ballistics matched it to the dead officer's service pistol. As Eli said to Gabe, "It was a hell of a shot."

Also in January, Gabe received a piece of mail at his office. There was no return address on the envelope, and the note read, "You are going to be a father. I'm carrying your child, and all is fine. Please don't try to contact me. Love, Eloise." He was taken aback but realized that was the risk of not wearing a rubber. Gabe took the note out in back of the station to their trash barrel and lit it with his Zippo. He did not think about this again.

Dr. Eli and Ms. Shaw were married in the courthouse on Valentine's Day 1957, with Gabe and Betty in attendance. Gabe was Eli's best man.

On March 20, 1957, Betty St. John delivered an eight-pound baby girl, Catherine Ann, after both of their mothers. Gabe was a proud and happy father and husband. Life indeed looked very good.

Printed in the United States
By Bookmasters